PRAISE FOR VIVIAN AREND

"Vivian Arend does a wonderful job of building the atmosphere and the other characters in this story so that readers will be sucked into the world and looking forward to the rest of the books in the series."
~ *Library Journal*

"Steamy and sweet complete with a whole host of colourful side characters and enough sub-plots to get your teeth into. A fab read!"
~ *Scorching Book Reviews*

"There's a real chemistry between the characters, laced with humor and snappy dialogue and no shortage of steamy sex scenes to keep things lively. The result is an entertaining, spicy romance."
~ *Publishers Weekly*

I have honestly waited AGES for Vivian to return to her world of shifters and this new trilogy is just what the Romance Witch doctor ordered! The setting is beautiful, the characters are hilarious, and the best friends-to-lovers story never gets old...
~ *Romance Witch Reviews*

Arend offers constant action and thrills, and her characters are so captivating and nuanced that readers will have a hard time guessing who the villains really are.
~ *RT Book Reviews*

A full list of Vivian's print titles is available on her website

www.vivianarend.com

THE ALPHA'S OPTION

TIMBERWOLF LODGE
BOOK 1

VIVIAN AREND

This is a work of fiction. Names, characters, places, and incidents either are the product of the author's imagination or are used fictitiously, and any resemblance to any persons, living or dead, business establishments, events, or locales is entirely coincidental.

The Alpha's Option
Copyright © 2022 by Arend Publishing Inc.
ISBN: 9781990674389
Edited by Angie Ramey
Cover Design © Croco Designs
Proofed by: Manuela Velasco & Linda Levy

All rights reserved. No part of this book may be used or reproduced in any manner whatsoever without written permission except in the case of brief quotations.

1

————

*J*ace Carter crested the top of the ridge and then eased on the brakes. The valley stretched out before him, a mix of late-spring green and shimmering-lake blue. A quick pause was all he wanted, to reminisce and get his head on straight before doing the next thing.

Thumbing its nose at the sentimentality of the moment, the engine of his borrowed truck rumbled unevenly, coughed twice, and stalled out.

He mumbled a curse, crawling from the cab to get a better view of the reason he was outside Jasper, Alberta.

Timberwolf Lodge. Memories rushed in—

Summer vacations with his extended family. Lazy days floating on the lake with his cousins, his childless Auntie Rachel and Uncle Jim acting as pack parents for whoever came out that year.

Jace's last summer there had been after college. The six years that had passed could have been sixty judging by the obvious neglect that greeted his gaze.

A kilometer below at the base of the hill, the lodge and

cabins dotted the lawn between the edge of the lake and the tree line that was the wilderness. The entrance of the main building still oozed grandeur. Enormous wooden beams stretched skyward over the double-sized front door, creating an A-framed central staging area that could have challenged a castle for imposing first impressions. The three wings of the lodge radiated out like spokes, with guest quarters and the living room/kitchen windows facing the lake.

But the wood siding was faded, the roof had seen better days, and weeds had taken control of the outdoor living spaces.

And Jace had all but been summoned here.

"What are you up to, Auntie Rachel?" He breathed in slowly, allowing the aromas of the area to fill his senses.

Huh. Someone was in the woods to his right. A second later, a branch broke, and Jace resisted the urge to roll his eyes.

An audible sigh hung on the air for a second before his cousin sheepishly stepped into view.

"Hey, Blue. Tie one on last night?" Jace asked. Should be the only good, or not-so-good, reason for the man's serious lack of stealth.

"I didn't want to surprise you." Somehow Blue kept from smiling. "Not everyone can handle being suddenly confronted by the wonder that is me." He drew a hand down his chest like a game show host displaying priceless jewels.

The dramatic effect showcased his tattered Hawaiian shirt and board shorts. The shirt, lime green. The shorts, pink with red-checked highlights.

Jace winced. "*Shock* is a better word for it. Staring at you is like looking at the sun. I'm going blind here, cuz."

"I have a matching outfit to this one if you'd like to borrow it."

Jace pretended to consider the offer seriously. "Generous, but let's not traumatize the locals more than you already do."

He extended his hand, clasped Blue's tightly, and pulled the other man into a warm embrace.

Blue sighed contentedly even as he pounded on Jace's back. "You've been gone a long time. Too long." He stepped back and glared. "I'm kind of pissed it took someone giving you property to get you to come home."

Jace shook his head. "Wildest thing ever. How was Auntie Rachel doing the last time you saw her? The only thing I heard was she'd mentioned wanting to travel."

Blue shrugged. "She lost interest in the lodge when Uncle Jim died."

Four years ago. How had things gone to hell so quickly? Jace's gaze landed pointedly on the neglected building.

His cousin raised his hands in protest. "Hey, I tried. I kept up with the maintenance she allowed, but even I couldn't sweet-talk her into letting me outright manage things for her. When she said no, she meant it."

True, there was no convincing a wolf who didn't want to change. Not while she was in her own territory.

Blue continued. "When she got all excited about the idea of traveling, I was happy to see it. She stopped by my workshop, nearly vibrating, about two months ago. 'So many plans,' she said. 'It was all coming together,' she said."

Jace dragged a hand through his hair. He'd gotten a call from the lawyers only four weeks earlier. "Two months ago?"

Blue considered. "Pretty certain. Oh, wait." His cousin dug into his pocket and pulled out an envelope. "Yup, see?

She dated it and told me to give it to you when you arrived. First thing."

Auntie's neat-as-a-pin handwriting shone up at Jace. Dated April 1, the envelope bore his name and Auntie's bold signature.

Jace opened it quickly then lifted the page so Blue could read it by his side.

Jace,

After Jim passed, I struggled to know what to do. Now inspiration has hit, and I know exactly what's needed. For me, for you, and your generation and more. Jim always wanted to make an impact in our community with Timberwolf Lodge. And now it will.

While I'm not dead, I don't expect to be back. Timberwolf needs to go on, and with no kids of my own, you won the lucky toss.
Congratulations. You'll thank me someday.

There are one or two small details to add. You own the property. You're the caretaker, so to speak. But the main house itself needs a woman's touch.

So I set up an online lottery and gave it away.

Jace pulled the letter a little closer and reread the last line. What?

She gave *what* away?

"She—" Was he confused and misunderstanding? "Did I read that right?" He stabbed a finger at the line where he'd stopped reading, because it had to be impossible.

"If you read that she gave you the property but gave the house to some random woman she found on the internet?" Blue made a quick *huh* noise. "Yeah, you read it right."

It was probably illegal on a dozen levels, but it was also the kind of family-jerking-family-around behaviour that, in most wolf packs, got cut a lot of slack.

They both leaned in closer to finish reading.

That's when the screams rang out. First a woman, followed by a deep, almost growling cry that echoed off the nearby mountains.

Jace ran, Blue hard on his heels. Down the path toward the weatherworn Timberwolf Lodge.

CASSIDY RUNDLE HELD a long broom in her hand, waving it as menacingly as possible at the Sasquatch-like figure standing three feet away. The man loomed over her, stark naked, in the middle of her new kitchen. He had an overabundance of hair covering him and a serious lack of anything else.

She poked the broom forward as if trying to brush him out the kitchen door. "Get out."

He folded his arms over his chest and raised a brow. The way he stared down the line of his nose clearly said he didn't consider her a threat. "No."

Drat. There were times she wished she were a whole lot bigger or at least a whole lot more armed. What was she supposed to do with a trespasser when all she had was a broom? Reason with him?

"I've called the cops." The warning rang out from behind Cassidy. "You should get out before they come."

After they'd innocently marched into the lodge and

discovered the intruder, Stephanie Nix—Cassidy's best friend, had retreated from the kitchen to the living room— and now stood in the huge front foyer. Stephanie had the over-sized front door wide open, which was good on all sorts of levels, Cassidy decided. It meant if they had to sprint for safety, there was a clear path to the great outdoors.

Mr. Hairy snorted. A big and totally amused sound. "Bullshit on that. There's no reception here."

Drat again. From the soft curses Stephanie mumbled at her back, Cassidy figured he wasn't pulling a fast one.

Cassidy tried again. "You need to not be here. You should probably put some clothes on as well. This is our house, but if you need help finding somewhere to relocate to, we would be happy to assist you with that."

"Once you have clothes on," Stephanie added.

The man yawned, stretching. Cassidy deliberately looked away from all things below his neckline, but it wasn't easy. He was a...*big man*...so to speak.

He opened his mouth, but whatever he was about to share morphed into a grunt of pain as something blue flashed past Cassidy and slammed into her trespasser.

The next second, a smear of fluorescent colours joined the pile, and then there were three burly men on the floor of her kitchen. The naked one cursed creatively, his voice a deep rumble.

Stephanie caught Cassidy by the arm and tugged her back. "Maybe now is when we step outside and double-check the paperwork. Because I don't remember this being part of the deal. The naked man and the wrestling."

Cassidy stood her ground, broom still firmly held toward the now non-squirming pile. Their naked trespasser was on the floor—facedown, thank goodness. One arm was pinned behind his back by a dark-haired man dressed in crisp new jeans. Mr. Nudie's legs were held down by a blond with surfer curls dressed in gaudy beach attire.

The dark-haired man swiveled his head toward her. "You okay?"

The jerk on the floor responded before Cassidy could. "She's fine. And the other one's got a set of lungs on her like an aspiring tuba player."

"She wasn't the only one we heard shouting," surfer dude taunted before patting his blue-jeaned friend on the shoulder. "I know Marvin. You want me to take care of him while you talk to the ladies?"

"Good idea," the man in blue said.

Cassidy didn't think so. "While I'm very happy to not be facing a potential safety risk, not to mention how unsanitary it is having a naked man in my kitchen, nobody is solving anything without me knowing all the details. This is my place—"

"—and mine," Stephanie inserted, attempting to suppress the quiver in her voice. "And I don't like naked or unsanitary people in my kitchen, either."

"Thank you, Stephanie. You're completely correct. It's your place too." Cassidy turned back to the three men who lay motionless like some strange Greek tableau. "If you will please *all* leave through the kitchen door. Anyone who is naked and wants to be part of the conversation can put some clothes on. We'll resume discussion by the firepit in five minutes."

She caught Stephanie by the arm, and the two of them retreated to the safety of their car.

Only after the doors were locked did Cassidy allow herself to rest her forehead on the steering wheel and take a steadying breath.

Stephanie went the other direction, tilting the seat back

as far as possible, which was not far considering the amount of stuff shoved in the back seat. She let her head fall against the headrest and sighed enormously. "Okay. That was unexpected."

Silence fell. Cassidy glanced at Steph to discover her friend peeking over at the exact moment. Lips twitched, then they both burst into laughter.

Amusement faded quickly, though. Everything about this situation was unexpected. "I guess winning an eco-lodge in a lottery is not without a few quirks."

Stephanie examined Cassidy, her bright blue eyes dulled with concern. "Is this going to work? Because this kind of has to work."

"It'll work," Cassidy assured her.

"Stacy needs somewhere for the kids, and I've already put all my money toward setting up a new spa here."

Cassidy laid a hand on her friend's arm. "It'll work. I promise."

Even if Cassidy had to sell her soul to make that happen.

All three of them needed something new and positive in their lives. While the lottery to win the lodge had seemed too good to be true, actually winning was even stranger. For better or worse, they'd done the four-day drive, and now they were here in Jasper, and this was where they were staying.

Cassidy stiffened her spine and lifted her chin. "You okay to come talk to them, or do you want me to do it by myself?"

Steph shook her head. "I'm coming with you. I represent not only me but Stacy as well, so I'd better suck it up and do this thing." She paused, opened the glove box, and pulled out a narrow metal tube she popped into her pocket. "Now I'm ready."

Cassidy grinned. "Please don't use that bear spray on anybody unless you absolutely need to."

"Then they better not mess with us. Because I'm armed and not afraid to use it." The evil glint in her friend's eye said she wasn't kidding.

To tell the truth, at this point, neither was Cassidy.

2

The women were gone before Jace had time to say another word. Which was good on one level because everything in him had shot to high alert, and not only because there were random people in his auntie's house.

The scent of *her* lingered—the petite brunette with the attitude and the killer legs—and his wolf sat up and paid attention.

Not right now, Jace warned himself. *Don't get distracted when there's still a potentially dangerous situation to deal with.*

Thankfully, the brute of a man he and Blue had pinned to the ground didn't throw up a fuss. "You gonna get off me sometime, or are we going steady now?" he grumbled.

Blue gave the man a slap upside the head as they all rolled to their feet. "What the hell, Marvin?"

Jeez, the man was a big bruiser. Definitely a shifter, although it took a moment for Jace to figure out what kind. "Why is there a moose shifter in Auntie Rachel's lodge?" he asked Blue.

"From what the ladies were saying, it's their lodge, and he's a squatter." Blue jerked his thumb toward Marvin.

"Am not." Marvin's indignation was sincere. "Rachel owed me a favour. Said I could live here for as long as I want, and I still want. Doesn't matter that she's taken off for parts unknown. She made me a promise."

Jace pointed to the kitchen door then paused. "You got clothes anywhere nearby, or are you living au naturel all the time these days?"

Marvin tilted his chin toward the small door off the hallway. "If you must know, I was doing laundry. It's easier to wash everything at once. Plus, it's not as if there's been anybody around to complain about me letting it all hang out."

A soft snicker escaped Blue. "Jace. You're already pinching the bridge of your nose. Obviously, this is going to be all sunshine and roses for you, the whole caretaking thing."

Dammit. Blue was right. It was a bad habit and a terrible tell.

Jace moved his fingers higher and rubbed at his forehead before taking a deep breath and looking Marvin in the eye. "Get dressed, then get your ass outside. The ladies are human, so we've got to come up with a solution that works for everyone, understand?"

Marvin sighed as if extremely put-upon. "I'm not a child."

"That's obvious from the hair. Damn, man, I have a spare razor I can loan you," Blue muttered before dancing out of reach of Marvin's massive fist.

Outside the kitchen door, Jace faced a wild combination of good memories and sadness. The enormous firepit where they'd spent many pleasurable evenings was still there.

Uncle Jim would play his guitar. Friends and family would sing along in either human or wolf form.

But now none of the little touches that had been Auntie Rachel's work remained. No twinkling fairy lights, no citronella torches. Weeds were everywhere, and a huge collection of beer cans was stacked in the shape of a castle beside the firepit.

Blue stopped and looked down at the recycled art. "I had no idea Marvin was still here."

"And it seems he intends to carry on." Jace glanced around again. The main lodge held space for group dining and entertainment along with a dozen rooms in two separate guest wings. But there were also multiple cabins scattered over the property.

Possible solutions began to percolate in his mind.

The sound of car doors closing brought Jace back to attention.

"Are you able to step in around here?" he quickly asked his cousin. Blue was an Omega wolf, which meant he held a separate place in the pack hierarchy. Spending time with Jace wouldn't put Blue at risk, but it was important to Jace that his cousin made the choice himself and wasn't pushed into it.

Blue nodded slowly. "I have two or three small projects I'm committed to at the shop, but if you're talking about helping to fix up this place long term, I'm your man."

"Want to live here or in town?"

His cousin frowned. "Pain in the ass to commute back and forth. And my rooms above the shop aren't nearly as nice as what I could organize here. As long as the new lodge owners agree."

Which was pretty much what Jace figured.

The women rounded the corner of the house. The door of the kitchen opened as Marvin stepped out, fully dressed and carrying a bundle of clothing.

Quickly, before the two groups joined them, Jace nodded firmly. "Okay. I'm still not sure what the hell Auntie Rachel was thinking, but we'll make it work. I'll find a way to fix it."

Blue rested a hand on Jace's shoulder. "That's what you do."

Yes, it was. God help him.

Jace had spent years building his own company. Carter Wells was making a huge difference in the world, providing inexpensive sources of fresh water to remote communities. But now instead of being full-time CEO and all that job description entailed, here he was. Thrust into juggling his work and the position of mediator and caretaker because of his aunt's wishes.

There wasn't time for this distraction. It made no sense for him to drop everything and return to Jasper. And yet, he'd never even considered ignoring the summons to come deal with her estate.

So be it, he thought. It was part of being a wolf. Though he hadn't been in the Jasper pack for many years, it appeared he was going to be now.

He hoped his cousin Del wouldn't be an ass about that decision.

THERE WAS something reassuring about having Stephanie at her back, armed and dangerous. Recalling the quick research she had done prior to heading west for this adventure, Cassidy positioned herself upwind of the three men standing beside the firepit.

If anybody was going to be hit by pepper spray, it wasn't going to be her or her bestie.

She did note with approval that the handsome man in blue strategically put himself between her and the dressed-but-still-massive trespasser.

Now that they were face-to-face, she took a moment to truly look at their rescuers—although she and Steph had been doing fine on their own, thank you very much.

The jean-clad one was obviously in charge. Medium length dark brown hair. Midnight-blue eyes that looked straight at her as she continued her perusal. His square jawline supported a face with generous lips and a slightly angular nose. Unlike his friend, who was dressed in hippie chic at best, this one wore a neat flannel shirt over a pair of brand-new Levi's.

When he held out his hand, she took it, and a sudden jolt passed from his fingers to hers. Not an electric shock, not an obnoxiously tight squeeze, but *something* all the same. Charisma? Magnetism?

He carried himself as if there was unlimited power hidden inside his muscular package.

"Jace Carter." He shook her hand then immediately greeted Stephanie as well. "This is my cousin, Blue."

"Cassidy Rundle. Nice to meet you, I guess."

Blue snickered and then turned it into a cough, wiping at his mouth to hide his smile. "Yeah, we get it."

The big man in the back didn't bother to offer a hand. He lifted his chin. "I'm Marvin. I live here."

A sudden gust of breath escaped Marvin as Blue casually leaned out with an elbow and struck him in the gut.

Stephanie sucked in air and took a half step back, hand slipping into her pocket.

Cassidy laid a hand on her friend's arm reassuringly before raising a brow at Blue. "Maybe we can hold off on any more physical violence and use our words."

"She's right. Blue, lay off. Marvin—" Jace lifted a hand and pointed at the big man who had just opened his mouth. "Shut it. We'll figure something out, but you are a big part of the current problem."

"This has got to be a misunderstanding," Stephanie said. "We own Timberwolf Lodge."

Jace made a circling motion with his hand. "Let's talk about that. I believe you," he hurried to reassure them before Cassidy could complain. "I'm a little shy on details."

Okay. This was doable. Cassidy patted her pocket, reassured that the copy of the paperwork was there and real. "A few months ago, I saw a message on social media about a wilderness lodge in the Jasper area being given away. An older woman talked about all the things she and her husband had accomplished but now that he was gone, she couldn't do it on her own. She didn't want to sell the place to some big conglomerate. She wanted it to go to people who would really appreciate it."

Jace nodded encouragingly.

Cassidy shrugged. "It caught my attention. I was in a dead-end job. Stephanie needed a change, and her sister had to—" She glanced at Stephanie. Then back at Jace. "Well, never mind that. But we thought it was a neat idea. We've seen shows about stuff like this on Netflix before, and they were legit, so I entered the lottery."

"Two weeks later this lawyer shows up on our doorstep with all the paperwork," Stephanie said. Colour had returned to her cheeks, and she spoke with confidence now.

"We gave notice on our apartment, sold what we didn't want, and came here determined to meet the requirements."

Blue eased a little closer to Stephanie, his posture relaxed. "You got requirements? And just so you know, this place was owned by our auntie, which is why we're involved."

That was a helpful bit of information. "Good. That means you guys will know who the caretaker is. Because, frankly, this place is a lot more run-down than we expected." She stiffened her spine as she raised a hand. "But, like Stephanie said, we *are* going to meet the requirements. According to the paperwork the lawyer gave us, we have one year to get the lodge up and running."

Jace glanced around and then winced. "Is there some monetary target you have to reach to prove you've accomplished that?"

"There's a board that has to approve," Stephanie offered. "The Wilson Pack, whatever that is. I think it's an environmental assessment group."

Jace lifted a hand to his face before redirecting his fingers to brush them past his nose and forehead and drag them through his hair. "Okay. That makes a lot of sense."

"That's good, but you still didn't answer my question," Cassidy pointed out. "Caretaker?"

Blue's grin stretched from ear to ear. He reached over and patted a hand firmly on Jace's shoulder. "Here's your man."

Drat. On one level, the news was a good thing. Jace was easy on the eyes, and Cassidy wouldn't mind having him around to look at. But nothing she'd seen since driving up to the place had left a good impression of his work ethics.

She met his gaze straight on. "Do you suck at your job on purpose?"

His expression grew long-suffering while both Blue and Marvin laughed heartily in the background.

Jace shook his head. "I'd tell you it isn't my fault, but I'm not sure you'd believe me. Let's talk about how we go forward and make this work."

"And I still live here," Marvin offered up. "Are we going to get to that part of the discussion now? Because I'm pretty sure Rachel would have included that in whatever she did. Mischievous old coot or not, when she said a thing, she did a thing."

Crap. Cassidy pulled the papers from her pocket and scrambled through them. "There was something."

Beside her, Stephanie made a soft sound. "Oh no. Is *that* what that means?"

They'd checked over the paperwork multiple times. Cassidy had thought the line about existing contracts meant something about not cancelling any bookings.

She found what she was looking for and read it out loud. "All terms are dependent on the expectation that the new owners will honour any previous promises and commitments Timberwolf Lodge has made to certain individuals."

She glanced up into the big hairy man's face. "You live here because Rachel said you could?"

He smiled back, his rather frightening visage turning strangely pleasant, despite all the hair. "I do."

So. They had their first guest.

Cassidy glanced at Stephanie, who simply shrugged. "As long as he keeps his clothes on, and maybe obeys a few more rules, we'll make it work."

It seemed that was going to be their forever motto. *We'll make it work.*

Cassidy met Jace's eyes. "I hope you're ready to dig in

and get messy because we plan to make this the best eco-lodge in the area. We're going to beat that requirement date and get the Wilson Pack approval. And you're going to help us."

There was amusement in his eyes but also acceptance. He dipped his chin. "As you wish."

3

———————

*H*e wasn't sure why it had taken this long for it to register. Jace could probably explain his initial slowness on the fact they'd been dealing with Marvin, pinning him to the floor and all that.

It wasn't until they were outside by the firepit and he got a closer look at Cassidy that he put the pieces together.

She smelled delicious. That was the first and brightest detail that made all the other warning signs start flashing. She had an attitude, which he liked. Good-looking, with lots of curves and muscles in all his favourite places. Oh, everything lined up nicely for him to be very attracted to Cassidy Rundle.

Being attracted to a human wasn't a problem in the big picture, but it was usually a lot easier when they were people who had grown up in the community. Not ones who came from the big city and might have never heard of shifters before.

The longer she talked and the more determined she proved herself to be, the more trouble Jace realized he was in. It wasn't only attraction he felt.

It was *the* attraction.

He wasn't going to help her achieve her dream—he was going to be right by her side the entire time. If his wolf had any say.

Thankfully, the women took a break and went into the house before Jace could do something unwise, like lean in and lick Cassidy from the base of her neck up past her ear, just to get a good solid taste of her skin.

Standing beside Jace as the ladies vanished behind the door, Blue shuffled from foot to foot, a grin on his face as he casually whistled toward the sky.

Frack. "What?" Jace demanded.

Blue shrugged innocently. "Oh, nothing. Nothing at all." He turned his attention on Marvin. "While I would never dream of taking charge of the situation over fair Cassidy, let's figure out a compromise before they come back. Rachel said you could stay, so you can stay. Where could you live other than the house that would make you happy?"

Marvin gazed into the forest as he thought for a moment. "To show what a considerate man I am, I'll say Cabin 7 is nice. That one's a studio. It's currently got a bit of a leak in the roof." He grinned at Jace. "I'm pretty sure a good caretaker can fix that up lickety-split."

Of course the caretaker could. "Very considerate of you to leave the larger cabins for *paying* customers."

"Considerate is my middle name," Marvin drawled, scratching his back against the nearest tree. He straightened then wiggled his shoulders. "I'm hungry. All the moving and shit can happen tomorrow. I need to forage."

Jace held up a hand. "Cabin 7 backs onto the woods. Shift only when you're out of sight of the house. And when

I come over to fix the roof, I'm going to make a fence so you can strip down and stay out of sight. Got it?"

"You have far too big a stick up your ass," Marvin said without heat, then walked away without agreeing to anything.

Jace's headache kept getting bigger, and it was barely even nine o'clock. "Think he'll listen to a word I said?" he asked Blue.

"Only if he feels like it."

They stood and waited until Marvin was out of earshot, then Blue whirled on Jace. "Seriously, we've got trouble."

Trouble or something to be celebrated, only Jace didn't know which they should handle first. "You think?"

"It was all I could do to keep from jumping her right then and there," Blue said softly, leaning in as he eyed the back door, likely to make sure the women weren't around.

A flash of anger struck Jace, hard and fast. Blue was drooling over Cassidy? The wolf had a death wish. "Really?"

Blue took an unsteady breath, breathing in deep. "God. She smells like fresh-baked bread and cookies, and I want to tumble her in the sack for hours."

This couldn't be happening. "You think she's your mate?"

"Whoa, dude. I thought you had the best sniffer around, but it's clear that when it comes to one-on-one fated attractions, I hit the jackpot, and you're out there in sad and lonely-ville."

Jace held on to his temper by a thin thread. He liked Blue, he reminded himself. He didn't want to rip out his cousin's throat. Yet it was becoming a close thing. "And what do you plan to tell Cassidy—"

"Cassidy?" Blue jerked to a stop and looked utterly

confused. "And why are you growling at me and suggesting such inane..."

They stared at each other for a moment before sighing heavily in relief.

"Well, the good part is you're not going to eviscerate me because, hell no, I'm not talking about Cassidy. I'm talking about Stephanie. She's the most glorious thing I have ever scented in my entire life." Blue grinned. "And it appears your bachelor days are coming to an end as well. Go us." Blue held his hand in the air and waited for a high five.

Unfortunately, Jace had a few other things to worry about before celebrating too hard. "Yeah. Awesome. The finding-my-mate thing is pretty good, but there's a complication."

"Can't compare to finding our mates," Blue insisted.

"No? The last time we spoke, I was told he'd hamstring me and then gut me if he ever saw me again. Which is a *tiny* bit of a complication."

Blue cursed. "Oh. You mean cousin Del."

"Uh-huh." It truly was a nightmare waiting to happen. Of all the things Jace hadn't wanted to deal with, his cousin Del was number one on the list. "Alpha of the Jasper pack. The pack affiliated with the Wilson pack, the one Cassidy and Steph need approval from in order to keep auntie's lodge."

STEPHANIE STARED OUT THE WINDOW. "They're still talking. Wait—that big moose of a man wandered off. Do you really think we're okay with him around?"

"We'll get solid reassurances of that, trust me." Cassidy laid her hand on Stephanie's arm. "I promised

Stacy that she'd have somewhere safe to bring the kids, and I meant it. This is going to be their home as well as ours."

Stephanie leaned in to make sure Marvin kept moving. "I know. I trust you. I always have."

They turned to each other, and the next minute, Cassidy was being squeezed in a huge hug. Stephanie's way of showing affection or comfort always involved hugs.

"Oh, stop. You're getting all emotional and icky on me," Cassidy complained.

"You lurve me. I know you do."

Cassidy made a gagging sound, which sent Stephanie into giggles like Cassidy knew it would.

She squeezed her friend once more because that's what Stephanie needed, then squared her own shoulders. "Okay, not everything has gone to plan. But at least we found the first glitches in the system, and we're going to get them straightened out. And we do have a caretaker, so I'll take that as a plus."

"He's cute," Stephanie noted. "And he likes you."

"Do you want me to gag again?" Cassidy asked.

"And I mean he's cute in a way that *you* like, not the way that I like. He has dimples." Stephanie leaned toward the window and looked in the other direction. "Now about that one. I don't know what kind of name *Blue* is, but he's entertaining."

"He's a bright spot of sunshine in an otherwise drab world," Cassidy agreed.

Stephanie held up a hand. "But, to reassure you, I am not looking for any kind of a relationship for however long it takes to get Timberwolf Lodge up and running. *That* is my priority. For you and Stacy and the munchkins."

Cassidy glanced out the window and caught Jace

looking at her. The intense connection between them struck again. "I know."

"Doesn't mean you can't have some fun," Stephanie whispered before pretending to cough and pat herself on the chest. "Oh my. I don't know where that came from."

Cassidy smiled and wrapped an arm around Stephanie's shoulders before guiding her back toward the outdoors. "That came from the core of you because you're the bluntest person on the entire planet, and I don't expect you to turn that off. Be yourself. We both deserve some fun. I'm certainly not going to ding you if you decide there's something you want to explore."

Stephanie placed a hand against the door before Cassidy could pull it open. "Unlikely, but right back at you, Miss My Lady Bits Are About to Fall Off from Lack of Use.'"

Cassidy raised a brow. "Please, I know how to masturbate just fine, thank you. There is no lack of anything in this vicinity."

"But you don't enjoy self-love as much as sex."

Stephanie spoke as they pushed the door open and made their way back outside. Both Blue and Jace waited attentively, visibly fighting to keep their expressions serious.

Cassidy had the eerie feeling that they had heard at least part of her and Steph's most recent conversation.

Whatever. Sex was fun, entertaining, and something she was allowed to enjoy. Only not right now when there was a falling-down building to get ready for business.

Jace stepped forward before she could meet them by the firepit. "This may be easier done inside if you've got something we can write with. Have you had a chance to look around the place yet?"

Cassidy shook her head. "We unlocked the door, came in, and—"

"—got an eyeful." Stephanie finished. "I have notebooks in my bag in the car. Want me to grab one?"

Cassidy nodded.

"I'll come with you." Blue damn near skipped up to join them, slowing as he approached Stephanie, who had retreated slightly behind Cassidy. "Sorry. I'm really good at lifting things. Just want to be helpful."

"It's okay. I'm a little jumpy after discovering a naked man in our house."

"He won't try that anymore," Blue promised as he gestured around the side of the house. "After you."

Stephanie patted her pocket then smiled. "Okay."

Cassidy kept from rolling her eyes, barely, as Stephanie and Blue paced out of sight.

"What's she armed with?" Jace asked quietly, a grin hovering on his lips. "Not that she'll need it. Blue is like the biggest puppy dog ever."

"Sometimes puppies get swatted on the nose with a newspaper so they learn not to nip," Cassidy pointed out as she led Jace into the kitchen. "She'll be fine. But I'm holding you to that. Not only Blue but our unexpected guest, Marvin."

"I promise they'll both behave."

The statement came out low and husky. She turned to discover him staring at her ass. She folded her arms over her chest, but that didn't help much because his gaze rose higher and lingered.

Drat, it was almost as if his hands were on her, a smooth caress over her skin then down between her legs.

Before she could call him on being rude, though, his

gaze snapped to hers. He looked uncomfortable. "Sorry. I *also* promise to behave."

She closed the distance between them and hooked her fingers into his belt. The close eye contact allowed her to watch his pupils dilate.

It had to be travel fatigue. It had to be something to do with the mixed-up chaos of the past months and weeks and days.

Because what she was thinking came out of her mouth. Just like that. *Pop*.

"What if I give you permission to misbehave?"

And she went up on her toes and pressed their lips together.

4

———————

*H*er taste flooded in, and his ability to think rushed out. Her lips were soft and smooth against his, not sticky with flavoured gloss that interfered with her taste.

He curled his hands into fists and rested them on her hips because his first instinct was to shove one hand into her hair and pull so he could totally consume her mouth. His other hand could then effortlessly slide underneath the sweater she wore until the weight of her breast filled his palm.

If he'd had any doubts, they were now eradicated. This was his mate, and no matter how impossible the next days were going to be, he didn't give a shit. Knowing she was his was enough. Convincing her of that fact wasn't going to be a hardship, but a privilege.

Cassidy jerked his shirt out of the way and pressed her cool palms to the heat of his belly. He gasped, stealing the air from her lips. He kissed her harder, leaning into her, somehow keeping his hands to himself.

"Jace," she murmured. "Touch me."

Thank God.

He slid one hand to her lower back and the other into her hair, tugging her head back and kissing his way over the line of her jaw and down her throat. He breathed deep, a ripple shaking his entire body as her scent flooded him. The hand at her back kept them sealed together, and his thick hardness pressed against the softness of her belly.

God, he ached. Craved to pick her up and take her against the wall. Or maybe find enough finesse to search the upper rooms and see if one still had a working bed.

The front door squeaked open. Cassidy stilled and then jerked her hands out from under his shirt. He let her go as she stepped away, her hands flying up to her heated cheeks.

Jace casually tucked his shirt back in as he twisted and pretended to examine the kitchen cabinets. "They probably only need a paint job."

Cassidy was still breathing heavily. She blinked hard before clueing in and nodding. "Sounds good. Paint and some cleaning. Yes, I think that's all this room needs."

She turned, all businesslike, toward where Stephanie and Blue stood in the living room.

Stephanie triumphantly held up a giant Post-it notepad. "Look. We can do some master planning. I'm excited."

Good. They'd managed to get away without the friend figuring out he and Cassidy had just been lip-locked.

One glance at Blue said Jace wasn't going to be nearly so lucky on that front.

His cousin outright grinned as he marched forward and put his armload of business supplies on the lone table in the room. "Making a list of tasks sounds like a great idea. Cassidy, I was telling Stephanie I'm a woodworker. Any renovations or furniture you need for the lodge, that's something I can help with."

"Good to know. It looks as if we need to make a master list, yes?" Cassidy whirled, turning her back on Jace as she marched over and snatched up a notepad and a pen. "Let's get going."

"I know the place, so I can guide you around," Blue offered. "Jace will take notes for us."

Such a jerk. One of Jace's least favourite things. "Let me take care of that."

Which meant he spent the next hour wandering after the trio of Blue, Stephanie, and Cassidy. Working really hard not to trip when it was all he could do to keep his eyes off Cassidy's ass and not to replay their first kiss over and over.

They'd just stepped out of the third small cabin when Cassidy gestured to the Adirondack deck chairs on the front porch. "Let's sit. I have some questions."

Stephanie dropped into the first available spot and pulled a water bottle from her oversized purse. "How come it looks as if no one's stayed here for a long time?"

"That's what I want to know. Because I assumed, from the way Rachel spoke in her videos, that Timberwolf Lodge had been a viable resort for many years. What happened?" Cassidy focused directly on Jace as she asked.

That damn guilt struck again. Still, he wasn't about to admit it had been years since he'd stepped foot on the place. "Her husband died. You said she mentioned that in the video before she set up the lottery."

Cassidy dipped her chin slowly. "Are you telling me no one has stayed here since he passed?"

"Other than the moose?" Stephanie said dryly. She snickered when Blue stiffened. "Okay, I know it's not nice to call people names even when they're not around, but it fits. He's so big, and he lumbers. Don't you agree?"

"No argument from me," Blue said. "But to answer the other part of your question, Cassidy, it happened slowly. The lodge had a lot of repeat customers from previous years, and they all came out the year after Jim died. But Auntie Rachel's heart wasn't in it anymore, so the experience wasn't the same. They eventually stopped coming."

"That's sad. Not only for her but for the people who used to vacation here." Cassidy's gaze drifted over the landscape and the cabins. Drifted over the lodge itself, which once had been a landmark of holiday happiness, yet it was now faded to a ghost of its former self. "I'll admit this entire project is more work than I thought it would be. Fortunately, the bones are there. It's got some charm."

"Maybe Blue and Jace know the people who used to come on the regular," Stephanie suggested. "We can get part of the place up and running then invite them back. A warm audience is always easier than starting from nothing."

It was a brilliant idea except for one thing. All those repeat visitors would be shifters, and right now Jace wasn't sure how to deal with *that* entire situation.

Damn it, Auntie. What were you thinking?

~

Something was up.

Something other than Cassidy's libido going into overdrive and causing her to behave in a reckless manner.

It was the way Jace and Blue hesitated before answering the simplest of questions as if rewording things in their heads. She'd seen enough of it in the past to recognize evasion. Now she had to figure out why it was happening.

Also, at some point, she had to decide whether she should totally ignore the fact that she had kissed Jace's brains out a short while ago or if she wanted to do something more about it. Do it again, even.

Decisions, decisions.

First, though, there were other priorities to knock off the list.

"First, thanks for strong-arming Marvin into taking Cabin 7, and don't try and tell me you didn't, because I know you did," Cassidy said pointedly at Blue when he opened his mouth to protest. "Next, I think we need to concentrate on fixing the main areas of the house and a couple of the cabins first. The house is where the meals will be served and the group gatherings will happen, but the private cabins will be a better sell for overnight guests. You can make a list of what that's going to take, Jace. Also, list any tasks that Stephanie and I can help with to move the project along faster. We should make a calendar."

"That's a great plan." Jace was still taking notes, but he glanced at her, and his eyes shone with approval. "Good to know you're willing to get your hands dirty."

"This is all or nothing," Cassidy told him. "Oh, I need you to include an estimated budget. Stephanie will have to pick one of the rooms or a cabin to set up a spa because that's her gig. Also, Steph's earlier idea was a good one. I'd appreciate if, despite whatever's making you hesitate, you and Blue could come up with a few names of people who would like to come back to Timberwolf Lodge. Starting small is a good idea, but at some point, we'll need money coming in instead of just going out. The account balance that your aunt included with the one year challenge was generous, but not limitless"

"Budgets are good, if annoying," Blue agreed. He hit Stephanie with another shot of puppy-dog adoration before pulling on a more businesslike expression. "If that offer of sweat equity applies to the new furniture you'll need for the lodge and cabins, I'm pretty sure I can work out some discounts."

"You're so sweet." Stephanie reached over and patted his cheek.

Blue flushed red as a ripe tomato.

"I'll think on that list," Jace promised. He cleared his throat. "I assume you ladies want to live here in the house? And did I hear mention of kids?"

Cassidy thought back but couldn't remember when she possibly would've mentioned that within their earshot. Still, it was absolutely true—no use denying it. "Stephanie's sister will be joining us by the end of the month. Stacy is a single mom, so they'll be here once the kids get out of school. The boys are ten, six, and five. Which is another reason I need to know for sure our guest in Cabin 7 will behave himself."

"Marvin will not be a problem around the kids. I can guarantee that," Blue offered immediately. "I know he didn't show up in the best light today—"

"Oh, the lighting showed everything just fine," Steph said with a dry snicker.

Blue's lips twitched. "But Marvin's only an ass to grown-ups. He thinks kids are the best."

A thoughtful gaze came into Jace's eyes. "The back wing of the lodge was the residence for my aunt and uncle, along with any help they had around. That could be set up as family quarters for Stacy. It's a bit more separated for the kids with more privacy when you have paying guests. Or they can take a cabin. You may want to check with her and see what she'd prefer."

Which was a thing Cassidy hadn't considered. "Good idea. Thanks for that."

Something crashed in the bushes loudly enough to make Cassidy jolt.

Stephanie shot to her feet and marched to the edge of the porch. Her fingers tightened on the railing. "Holy shit."

Cassidy joined her, jaw dropping open as the biggest moose she'd ever seen in her life—okay, the first moose she'd ever seen in real life—marched past her SUV. "Good Lord. Do we need to shoot him or something?"

"Tempting," Blue muttered.

Jace coughed but joined them at the railing. He smiled reassuringly. "It's okay. He's just wandering around the territory. If he becomes a bother, I'll make sure he's relocated."

"Are there other wild animals we'll see around here?" Stephanie asked rather breathlessly, staring after the moose until he disappeared down the road and into the ravine.

"The usual. Quite a few predatory birds like eagles and hawks. Some of the bigger animals like moose and elk. There's a wolf pack in the area and the occasional bear." Jace said it matter-of-factly, but he was staring at Blue as if telling him to keep his mouth shut.

What was it with these two and their bro-eyes-staring secretiveness? It was starting to piss Cassidy off.

Still, she had another issue to deal with first. "We need groceries, and we need to eat before we hit the store to keep from making all sorts of unwise choices. Since you've been helpful, and since getting you to show us the way into town will make life easier, we'll take you for lunch."

Stephanie frowned. "Where's your vehicle, by the way?"

Blue pointed up the hill. "Jace's is up there. He's having a little problem with his carburetor."

Once again, wonderful. Cassidy eyed her new caretaker

with concern. "Please tell me you have the skills to do what we need around here?"

Jace raised a hand. "I solemnly swear I will take care of you."

The shiver that hit her shouldn't have happened. Also, he hadn't really answered her but gone in a completely different direction. Ridiculous how the silliest things he said sent her insides quivering. But so be it.

She would deal with the lust issue shortly. First, she needed to fill her belly.

They moved inside, where Blue helped Stephanie pack up the notebooks. "Barbecue sound good?"

"Oh, I don't eat meat," Stephanie deadpanned back. "Is there somewhere in town that serves tofu?"

Her delivery was perfect. Both Blue and Jace shuddered before fixing obviously fake smiles back in place.

"Sure," Blue said with a little less enthusiasm.

Stephanie ruined her game face by laughing. "Just kidding. Barbecue is wonderful, although I do like tofu as well."

"Tofu with barbecue sauce, I can do," Blue offered.

Cassidy turned to discover Jace right beside her. He was staring at her in a very heated yet not creepy way. "And what do you like, Cassidy?"

"Flavours. Sweet, salty, spicy enough to make your hair curl. I like food to be invigorating and the company to be entertaining."

He dipped his chin. "Then I know exactly where we're going. Blue? Call Pete and tell him to save us a booth."

Cassidy was too busy staring into Jace's mesmerizing eyes to be certain, but she was almost positive she heard Blue curse softly before saying, "Okay."

5

———

This was beyond foolhardy. Sheer and utter chaos.

Jace had left Timberwolf Lodge and the town of Jasper behind all those years ago on purpose. Leaving meant he'd avoided a war no one could win.

Being summoned back by his auntie's letter had him mentally scrambling for ways to keep the peace. Most of those required flying under the radar or never stepping foot in town. Ever.

He shouldn't be taking the ladies anywhere near Jasper, let alone into his cousin's restaurant.

But as he enjoyed the amazing feeling of his hand on Cassidy's lower back, guiding her to a table at Pete's, he somehow knew this needed to happen. Drat it all anyway.

It wasn't yet noon, so the place was only a quarter full, but already all eyes were on their group as Blue led them toward a corner booth.

Good—slightly out of view, a wall to put his back to...

"Jace, you old scoundrel. How the hell are you?"

Doomed. They were all doomed, Jace decided as he turned to face his Uncle Lenny. So much for a quiet reentry

35

into the wolf community. Jace wondered how long it would take for everyone to know he was there, considering Lenny was the loudest gossip in the entire pack.

How long before Del heard and decided to appear?

Nothing to do but roll with it, Jace realized. "Just fine, Uncle. Looking for a bite to eat, that's all."

Lenny grabbed Jace's free hand and shook it with wild enthusiasm. "Sure you are. Only place in town worth coming to, my Pete's place. Sit, sit. Everyone will be so excited you're back. Been a long while. Told everyone you'd walk right back through those doors someday. Who's this? She yours? Of course, she is."

Before Jace could insert himself between Lenny and Cassidy, his uncle had grabbed her hand and lifted it as if ready to press a kiss to her knuckles.

Cassidy twisted. A seemingly casual move that left Lenny bent over empty air while she stepped to the side and stopped in front of Stephanie, instinctively protecting her friend.

Jace noted with approval how Cassidy left her feet and arms free to kick or punch as necessary. A rush of lust hit him, and he wallowed in the sensation.

A sexy, sexy woman who knew how to protect herself and others? He was so fucking gone. It didn't matter that it had been only hours since he first laid eyes on her.

Such was the power of fated mates, he realized.

She was glorious, and he would do anything for her. Including save her from bruising her knuckles on his uncle's face, because that seemed to be next on the agenda and closing in fast.

Jace resumed his position close to her side but clearly left her in charge. "Cassidy, our uncle Lenny. His son owns the restaurant. Uncle Lenny, meet Cassidy. She and her friend Steph are the new owners of Auntie Rachel's lodge. Blue and I are working with them to help get the place up and running again."

"You're working with—" Lenny choked off, then took a deep sniff. He rolled his eyes before glaring at Jace, finally clueing in that Cassidy and Steph were human. "Well, *hell.*"

Cassidy folded her arms over her chest, disapproval oozing from her as she examined Lenny. Then she pointedly ignored the older man and turned to Jace. "Is there food planned soon, or should I go shoot something?"

Imagining her going out to hunt for herself turned him on all over again. "We'll sit. My uncle was just leaving."

Only, the table in the corner was now occupied.

There was no use in being secretive anymore. Jace pushed past his uncle and pulled out a chair at the table in the exact center of the room. Like teamwork, Blue held out a chair for Stephanie.

The two women sat smoothly as if there weren't dozens of eyes staring from every direction.

"Jace. Sit here," Cassidy requested, tapping the chair beside her. The one that put him with his back to the door.

To hell with it. He sat.

Blue's eyes widened, but he quickly took the other chair next to Stephanie.

Cassidy met the gazes of the pack members in the room as she leaned slightly toward him. "Interesting place."

"It grows on you," Jace said evenly.

"So does mold."

He laughed, twisting to face her. "It's the best food in town, though. And so you know, there are no menus. We'll get served whatever Pete is cooking today."

"And we'll like it?"

Blue was nearly drooling, his gaze following someone who approached the table from behind. "You'll be begging for seconds. I promise. Hey, Pete."

Pete himself stopped beside the table, an enormous tray balanced on his shoulder as if it weighed nothing. "I heard there was trouble in the room. Blue, always good to see you." He shifted his gaze, danced it over Jace, then examined the women. "Cassidy. Stephanie. My apologies for my dad. He's all piss and vinegar."

"Though hopefully not in the kitchen area," Stephanie offered with a straight smile. "Is that the food we're supposed to like or else?"

"Bonus points for speed," Cassidy muttered. "Hello, Pete. Jace said this was the place to be. We're ready to be dazzled."

"Dazzling is what they do at the art shop. I feed the soul." Pete examined them again. "Allergies?"

"None," Cassidy and Stephanie said in unison.

Pete lowered the tray and began dispensing food. "Good. Then if there's anything you don't want, tough. Try it anyway."

The entire place could blow up any minute if Del or any of the other leaders of the pack showed up, but right now, Jace decided to hell with worrying. Pete was handing out food, and his cousin was a magician in the kitchen.

The apocalypse could wait. Jace had lunch to devour.

None of this day had gone to plan, but by now, Cassidy was struck by a strange sense of satisfaction every time she dealt with another twist.

Naked man in her new house? No biggie.

A lodge that needed repairs after years of neglect? She could see a path forward on that one.

This restaurant with an odd greeting committee, far too many curious onlookers, and no menu? Okey-dokey.

A caretaker who had been absent for most of the past years—okay, that one she was going to hold Jace's feet to the fire for eventually.

Right now, though, she was obsessed with the mass of food Pete had dropped onto the table with a seemingly casual attitude but an intense gaze that screamed he was more interested in her reaction than he wanted to admit.

No problems there. She was tempted to shovel in giant mouthfuls as fast as she could, and only years of being a grown-up stopped her from being that rude.

Macaroni and cheese with mixed chunks of bacon cooked so perfectly, they melted on her tongue. A grilled cheese sandwich with a layer of a spicy-sweet jam. A soup spicy enough to make her sweat. And that was only what was in front of her.

Jace didn't blink when she reached over and stole another of his fries.

"Truffle oil and gorgonzola cheese," he told her after swallowing a bite of his enormous burger.

"So good," Cassidy said. Screw even attempting to be polite. She caught him by the wrist. "Can I try your burger?"

His pupils went huge. Instead of passing the burger over, he held it out and waited as she took a bite. His gaze fixed on her lips, and she got hit by hot and cold flashes even as the taste of the perfectly cooked burger exploded in her mouth.

She pulled back, but before she was out of reach, he lifted his other hand and wiped at a spot near her lips.

Instinctively, she turned and caught his finger in her mouth, licking the drip clean.

The hot and cold inside her swelled to volcano and iceberg status. His gaze never drifted, and all she could think about was kissing. She'd kissed him. Could kiss him again if she wanted.

Yes, please, with cherries on top.

Okay, that was an easy choice. She *would* kiss him again in the future because it was something she wanted. But for now…

"Try my pizza," Stephanie demanded, thrusting forward a piece.

"Try my onion rings," Blue offered.

Cassidy was going to have a food orgasm right there at the table. "Your cousin is amazing," she told Jace and Blue after accepting all the samples.

"Does this mean you've forgotten the issues with our uncle?" Blue asked.

"What issues?" Stephanie shoved Blue's hand away as he tried to snag another piece of her pizza. "Touch that and die."

"Trade you for a spicy meatball," he countered.

They were cute and obviously headed for a food coma.

Cassidy met Jace's gaze again. "Okay, as ideas go, Pete's place was a spectacular one. I forgive you for all the things you're not telling me. Or I will if you hand over the rest of your donair."

Jace's grin lit her up inside. "You may have my donair and my apologies for the secrets. I promise I'll tell you what I can, when I can. It's…complicated."

"That's what they all say."

"Sometimes it's even the truth." Jace scooped the rest of the deliciousness that was his donair onto her plate and then leaned closer. "Here's one truth I won't make you wait for. You're the sexiest woman I've ever met."

Oh, please. Did he somehow know she planned to kiss him senseless at some point in the future? "Thanks. But I'm not giving your donair back."

He grinned, those deadly dimples flashing again, and her heart gave a weird *thump-thump* that was over-the-top and outrageous. So be it. Food now. Renovations and lodge plans after. Seduction, or at least lip locking, later.

That was the extent of Cassidy's agenda until the unfamiliar blonde beauty walked up to their table out of the blue and sat herself on Jace's lap.

"Hey, darling. I heard you were back and rushed over to tell you how much I've missed you." The blonde pressed her hands to his cheeks and made a move to kiss him.

It had been one weird day. Cassidy admitted that readily. But for some reason, this was a step too far.

To his credit, Jace had thrown his hands up to break the grip between him and the newcomer. But even faster, Cassidy caught hold of the woman's ponytail and gave it a hard yank.

The motion jerked Blondie's lips away from Jace's.

The second jerk pulled the woman off his lap and sent her tumbling to the floor.

Blondie bounced, then moved to scramble to her feet, the look in her eyes warning she planned to lunge at Cassidy.

Nope. Cassidy still had food on her plate that she wanted to enjoy and having someone come to their table who was possibly all germy was beyond the pale. She shoved back her chair far enough to reach out a foot and step on the other woman's thigh, pinning her in place.

"Don't move," Cassidy said quietly. Heck, her tone was even friendly and all that. "Steph?"

"On it." The next minute her bestie was behind the blonde, and that's when the stranger's cursing really started. Like a rodeo cowboy, Steph moved in a wild yet precise rhythm, and seconds later, she threw her hands in the air with a satisfied grin. "Done."

Except for the cursing blonde, whose hands and feet had been zip-tied in award-winning time, the entire café was once again utterly quiet, all eyes on their table.

Okay, Cassidy's reaction had been extreme. She should feel embarrassed. Ashamed, even.

Nope, not even a little bit. The only thing that remained was a fine rumble of jealousy and fury that the bitch had dared sit on Jace's lap.

Embrace the weirdness of the situation, Cassidy decided.

She turned to Jace. "Someone you know?"

6

<hr>

Jace was so damn turned on at that moment.

It was all he could do to keep from grabbing Cassidy. If he hauled her across the distance between them, he could claim her right then and there. It was a bad idea on many levels but still very tempting.

It appeared the longer they hung out at Pete's, the more likely things would continue to escalate.

Jace made a calculated decision and ignored everyone except for Cassidy. He met her gaze as he laid a hand on her thigh. "Emma is an old friend. She forgot we were no longer a thing, but I'm pretty sure she remembers now."

Fire flashed in Cassidy's eyes. "Old friend. Suppose that means you want me to untie her."

Emma continued to mutter curses but was smart enough to not come right out and call *Cassidy* any names. Instead, she switched to insulting Jace.

"Damn jackass. Think you can leave and then march right back in anytime you please? Del is going to have something to say about that. And you'll deserve every bit of pain he gives you."

"I really don't want to untie her," Cassidy said bluntly, ignoring Emma and speaking directly to Jace.

"But if you do, we can ask her to leave. Hell of a lot quieter, and you can finish your lunch in peace."

Cassidy considered, then nodded. "Steph?"

The other woman had gone back to her seat on the other side of the table and was digging into both her food and the little that remained on Blue's plate. She waved a hand airily. "I tie assholes up. I don't set them free. Besides, I don't have anything to cut the straps with."

"I'll do it," Blue offered. He paused to point at Stephanie. "If you eat the last of my onion rings while I'm gone, we are going to have words."

He slipped over to where Emma was still fuming.

Jace watched all this in his peripheral vision because keeping eye contact with Cassidy seemed far more important. She really did have the prettiest eyes. A deep green with the faintest hint of gold around the irises. "Emma. You need to leave."

He put the slightest bit of dominance into the words, and the cursing stopped instantly. Interestingly, across from him, Cassidy's pupils dilated the slightest bit, and a hunger crossed her face that made everything in him sit up and take notice.

Oh, now that was interesting.

"I'm going to tell Del," Emma announced. Only she spoke far more politely this time, which was acceptable to his wolf.

"Good for you. Tell him my number is the same as always. If he wants to give me a shout, we'll talk."

Cassidy twisted her head to watch as Emma stomped her way out of the restaurant. "She's pretty, but that attitude would be tough to handle for any length of time."

Discussing old flames with his future mate was not happening. Ever. Jace ignored Emma completely. "Do we need to get Pete to bring us a dessert or two?"

It was like a spotlight turned back on him. Cassidy's one-hundred-proof smile burst out and made him want to roll over so she could pet his belly. "I think we'll finish what's on the table and get our dessert to go." She leaned in closer and whispered, "We need to have some of that secret-sharing conversation back at the lodge."

Which wasn't a bad idea.

Somehow they got through the rest of the food on the table while conversations slowly rose around them again. Jace met gazes with pack members who were, as far as he could remember, neutral in the situation. Most of them seemed curious rather than worried.

By the time Pete brought an enormous paper bag to the table, the plates had been all but licked clean.

He went straight to Cassidy. "This is for you."

Cassidy wrapped her arms around the bag greedily. She peered around it at Jace. "Did you hear that? All mine."

Pete exchanged glances with Jace and dipped his chin. Approval there, and acceptance. This was one quarter where he wasn't going to have any troubles, and Jace was grateful. Not only would he have missed Pete's cooking, but his eccentric cousin was rock solid. The exact type of wolf Jace needed on his side in the days to come.

Jace pressed a wad of money into his cousin's hand. "This is for the meal. Thanks for everything."

"Thanks for not starting a bloodbath in the restaurant," Pete said sincerely. "See you around?"

"I'm not going anywhere," Jace said clearly, rising to his feet. "I'll get your truck back to you when I can."

"Just don't drive it anywhere too remote," Pete warned. "She's been cranky lately."

Ha. He could have used the advice earlier. Jace took the bag from Cassidy, then offered her his hand.

Escorting her out with dozens of eyes on them somehow felt right. That was where she belonged, at his side. Him beside her.

Now to figure out how in the world to get there for real. Maybe when they got back to the lodge, they could sit down and have a simple discussion about some facts of life that, until now, Cassidy and Stephanie knew nothing about.

You know, sit down and explain how some people could shift into animals. How this was their way of life, and—

Yeah. Real simple.

But maybe it would be easy. Jace would be smart enough, though, to make sure there were no zip ties anywhere nearby and that both the ladies were fully sated on the desserts Pete had offered.

CRÈME BRÛLÉE CHEESECAKE with chocolate sauce and raspberries was now Cassidy's favourite thing in the whole entire world.

"Can we kidnap Pete and bring him here so he can cook for us?" Stephanie moaned as she brushed pecan pie crumbs from the front of her shirt.

"Kidnappings are usually disapproved of," Blue said.

"You're so mean."

"Oh, I never said I wouldn't do it, just making sure you understood how far I would go."

Blue and Stephanie offered each other grins and exchanged pieces of pie.

Jace had taken a single cookie from the bag and then sat back in the chair as if he were plotting world dominance while the rest of them consumed every single calorie out of the to-go bag.

Only Cassidy had been watching him. Mostly as he watched her. "I'd offer a penny for your thoughts, but I have a feeling they're worth more than that."

He dipped his chin slowly. "In that category of things we haven't been telling you because they're complicated. I'm trying to figure out how to uncomplicate a little bit without getting all of us in trouble."

"Because you're secretly in the Mafia," Stephanie guessed. "And if you tell us, you have to kill us?"

"Yes." Blue said it with an absolutely straight face.

It was the fact he didn't say anything else and just sat there staring at them that made his words seem far too ominous and real.

Jace sighed. "Stop it, Blue."

Blue straightened then winked at Cassidy. "But see, now that I did that, when I do *this*, you'll know to trust me. It is an awful lot like the Mafia, and there is the potential for death, but it wouldn't be yours, so you don't need to worry about that part."

"Blue." Sharper this time from Jace. A strange crack of power hit the room along with the scent that lingers after a lightning strike.

The other man sprawled lazily on the couch beside Stephanie, stretching out with his arms along the backrest. "Too bad your spooky voice doesn't work on me, cuz."

"You're not helping."

"And you're overanalyzing," Blue insisted. "They're going to understand."

"And you know this how? Because you've got some

magical sixth sense—" Jace started and then cut off suddenly. He pinched the bridge of his nose. "Okay. You do have some magical sixth sense to tell you these things. I'm sorry."

"No offense taken," Blue said cheerfully. "Do you want to start, or shall I?"

"You already started," Jace muttered.

Stephanie's gaze had been bouncing back and forth between the two men. "It's amazing how entertaining you two are considering you haven't said a single thing I can comprehend."

"Does this information you need to tell us have to do with Timberwolf Lodge? Because if yes, I'd really like to know sooner than later. Like in the next century," Cassidy offered.

"It only has to do with the lodge on one level. Maybe two." Jace frowned. "Okay, it's totally tangled together with the lodge. So, here's the thing. Our auntie, who gave you the lodge..." He shook his head. "No. Wrong place to start."

He glanced over at his cousin as if asking for help.

Blue shot to his feet and paced behind the couch. "See? I knew it. Even people at the top of the food chain can eventually learn."

"Yeah, yeah. Get on with it."

"This will be much easier with a demonstration. Consider me your live-action *what we're dealing with here* starting point, and Jace will fill in the gaps after that." He unbuttoned his shirt, slipped it from his shoulders, and hung it over the back of the couch.

When he proceeded to undo his button and fly and drop his pants, Cassidy decided she wasn't about to stop him. After all, what was another naked man in her house? Albeit in the living room this time instead of the kitchen.

Stephanie leaned back on the couch and peeked behind the backrest. "Want me to find some music? To help set the mood?"

By this time, Blue was naked. "Nope. This'll only take a minute."

Too bad Cassidy couldn't blame it on a sugar coma. But it was no hallucination. One minute Blue stood there, a prime example of manhood, and the next, a large wolf rounded the corner of the couch and sat on the floor by the coffee table. Head tilted to the side with the same cocky expression Blue had worn seconds earlier.

"Oh. Okay." Cassidy pinched her wrist and then glanced at Jace in the chair next to her. She wasn't totally clueless but seeing someone new do this same outlandish trick had sent a shot of adrenaline streaking through her. "You can get furry."

Stephanie's jaw hung open. "Seriously? Okay, let me do the math here. If you two are cousins, and it was your auntie who owned Timber*wolf* Lodge, then this place is, like, totally your 'family' home."

She put air quotes around the word *family*.

Blue panted, smiling directly at Jace.

"I hate you," Jace told him. "You're going to be impossible to live with."

The wolf yipped and grinned even harder.

Jace turned to Cassidy. "Not the reaction I expected. You know about shifters?"

She now better understood his *it's complicated* comment. "I do, but more in a rhetorical sense. Head knowledge and not actual how-it-all-works knowledge. You've still got some explaining to do, especially when it comes to you and your cousin Del and whatever big scary things seem to be hanging over all our heads."

Blue jumped up on the couch before resting his head on his paws as he stared at Stephanie.

"Can I touch him?" Stephanie swore softly. "Never mind. Forget I asked that way because it was totally rude. You're still you, although now you're annoyingly cute. Blue? Can I touch you?"

Blue wiggled forward on the couch until his chin rested on her thigh. A clear invitation.

While Stephanie reached out a hand and slowly caressed Blue's ear, Cassidy had an important question on her mind. She turned to face Jace. "And you can do this too?"

"Turn into a wolf? Absolutely, since I was about four months old."

That's what she figured based on her previous intel.

Which put the fact she had already been plotting to kiss him silly, and do more intimate things, into an entirely different category of Need to Think About.

For now, she simply nodded. Although she really wanted to ask him to show her. "That list of things we were talking about getting done for the lodge. Any of that need to be adjusted with this *you are furries* information in mind?"

He and Blue both winced. "Some, although FYI, we'd really rather you call us *shifters* and not *furries*. Those are something completely different. You want to talk about this now or get settled in first? Because the afternoon is going to pass quickly, and right now, you don't have anywhere to sleep."

It wasn't a bad suggestion. "If I sit here much longer, I'll go into nap mode. And you're right. There's a lot to do to make this place livable, even if it's only for us in the short term." She lifted a finger at Jace. "But this conversation is not over."

"Absolutely not," he agreed. His gaze drifted over her, heat there the same as before. "Let's get started on making this place into a home."

She wasn't sure why those words made her shiver with anticipation.

7

Not having to spend hours calming Cassidy and Stephanie down or talking them out from behind a locked door was a lovely surprise.

Blue gloating incessantly? Less lovely.

"I swear, if you grin at me like that one more time, I'm going to rip off your tail and shove it down your throat," Jace warned.

Blue *tsked*. "Okay, fine." He widened his eyes and set his teeth together in a lopsided fashion. "Like this grin better?"

Jace hit him. It was totally justified. The fact Jace was holding a bedside table, the weight of which struck Blue in the side and sent him sprawling to the floor, might have been a little rude, but still...

Mostly justified, Jace figured.

Blue picked himself up, still laughing. "Okay, I'll stop now, but seriously, cuz. Your face when they both barely blinked at the sight of my furry awesomeness was hysterical."

"I'm sure it was. But now we need to agree to remove

the word *furry* from our vocabulary because that's not something we want to become canon when discussing us, our pack, or werewolves in general, right?"

His cousin picked up the bed linens that had scattered to the ground when he'd fallen. "Right. So, when are you going to tell them the rest? Including the bit about you and Cassidy being...you know? Mates."

"I'm making this up as we go along, obviously." Jace placed the table beside the mattress they'd brought in from the storage shed. "What are you going to tell Stephanie?"

"Nothing."

Jace glared at him. "Blue. You're not thinking of keeping a secret from your mate, are you?"

"No, not really." Blue considered. "There's something still going on that I'm not clear on. As if I'm sure we *will* be mates but we're not mates yet, and something else has to happen before we can become mates. I'm okay with that."

Okay? Jace's insides shook from wanting Cassidy so much, and Blue was casually planning on not making the next move?

Omega wolves were so weird.

"You know, you're not right." Jace shook his head. "I mean, I know you're right for you, but damn..."

"I know, I know. We can't all be unicorns."

They stared at each other across the mattress for a moment. Family, but also friends from way back. There had never been a time when Jace hadn't trusted Blue. His cousin had always somehow been at the center of making things right, and even though they were both looking down the barrel of a pretty big gun, there was no reason to stop trusting now.

"One step at a time," Jace said firmly. "I may not have mystical woo-woo powers, but this much feels right. I will answer any question Cassidy asks, but I'm not going to leap ahead and throw everything on the table. The priority is finding a way to get Timberwolf Lodge up and running."

"Which means, now that we know *they* know about shifters, we can contact some of the old long-term summer residents." Blue looked thoughtful. "Although, we both know fixing up this place and getting contracts back on the books are minor details to the real problem."

Which would be the fact that by now Del would have heard Jace was back in town. "Still thinking of the best way to deal with that," he confessed.

Blue followed him into the hallway and down the stairs. "I take it this means you're not sticking with the status quo?"

Jace pulled to a stop in the kitchen, the sight out the window of Cassidy and Steph cleaning up around the firepit a sweet mixture of memories and hope for the future. "I can't. If this had only been a short-term visit, I would've kept my head down or even groveled to keep the peace. But she changes everything."

A hand landed gently on his shoulder. Blue nodded sagely, his wise and gentle expression completely incongruent with his outlandish clothing. "Mates *should* change everything. And while I can't absolutely promise everything will be hunky-dory, I will say I feel good about the coming changes."

"Drat, I hoped you'd had a vision of Del walking up, shaking my hand, and everything falling into place."

"Wouldn't that be nice?" Blue muttered. "I hope neither of you ends up missing body parts."

Jace was in full agreement, but it didn't change the truth. "I'll do what I have to. You know I don't want to fight Del, but if that's what it takes, I have no choice."

His cousin turned to face him, amusement rising in Blue's expression. "I hated when you left. I hated that you and Del nearly came to ripping out each other's throats more, so leaving was the right thing to do." Blue gestured toward where the women were now laughing. Stephanie wore a crown she'd made from pretty coloured weeds. "But now, thanks to our auntie, the players have changed. The ladies look right here. So, yeah, whatever it takes, I'm your man."

Blue thrust out a hand, and Jace took it. That connection between them flared bright—family and friendship and something instinctual, deep on the level of wolves, that made the floor beneath his feet seem a little sturdier.

Jace still had no idea what the timeline would be or the best way to go about it. He had to follow his own instructions.

One step at a time.

Outside the window, Cassidy attempted to move an oversized birdbath. Jace hurried toward the door, ready and willing to do whatever his mate needed. Heavy lifting, answering questions.

Hopefully kissing. And more.

Inside, his wolf stretched and perked up his ears.

And yes, sometime soon, he needed to introduce Cassidy to his other half.

THE REST of the day flew past in a blur of activity.

Their focus was on setting up two of the rooms with attached bathrooms, one for Cassidy and one for Stephanie.

They also began organizing and cleaning the living room and getting the kitchen in working shape.

Or, as Stephanie said, de-Marvinizing the space.

Somehow, in the middle of the work, Blue not only skipped out to the store but pulled together the fixings for a very small supper. Which was more than enough considering how much they'd consumed earlier in the day.

Some furniture in the house was at least temporarily usable. Some only needed elbow grease to be cleaned up. Between the two stuffed-to-the-brim bedrooms they discovered and the items in an outdoor storage shed, Cassidy could already picture what the lodge could look like in the end.

But the sheer amount of work needed to be anywhere near ready was exhausting to think about. Cassidy had a background in hotel and resort management but starting from the ground up was different. She needed to expand her plan and add a lot more details, especially after she got the rest of the information from the guys.

It was barely nine when Stephanie collapsed into a chair by the firepit, the back of her hand pressed dramatically to her forehead. "Stick a fork in me and call me done."

Blue settled beside her, holding out a water bottle that glistened with cool condensation. "Hydrate. If you haven't got your health, you haven't got anything."

Stephanie thrust her arm out in the air, fingers open, eyes closed, trusting Blue would move and meet her in the middle. "I'm almost too tired to appreciate the *Princess Bride* quote. Almost. Go, you."

"I aim to please."

Cassidy sprawled back in her chair, staring up at the still blue sky. "All these hours of daylight are pretty cool, but

I can see it being tempting to work way beyond what's reasonable."

"You did a good day's work," Jace said as he tended the fire, flames crackling over the wood.

"We did five days' good work in less than twelve hours," Stephanie corrected. She'd already chugged the entire water bottle and now stood with a groan. "Every party needs a pooper, and tonight, that's me. I did most of the driving the four days before this, and I am done. I'm going to soak in that freshly scrubbed bathtub and then crawl into my bed with the freshly washed sheets, and if you see me before noon, it's not really me. It's the ghost of me, looking for coffee."

Blue bounced to his feet. "I'll walk you to the house."

Stephanie eyed him. "Because it's so far." She glanced at the door less than twenty feet away, back at the fire, then at the door again. "How shall I find my way without your assistance?"

"I know where there's a hidden chocolate stash." Blue stood stock-still as Stephanie all but jumped at him. "I'll take that as a yes. Good night, Cassidy. Night, Jace. I'm going to run back to my place and pack up some things. I'll see you in the morning."

Her best friend and Jace's cousin disappeared into the house. A minute later, Blue appeared again, waved, and then sauntered off up the road. Hands in his pockets, whistling merrily as he walked into the forest.

"Huh."

Jace pulled one of the chairs closer to the fire before twisting so he faced Cassidy. "What's up?"

"Just a little confused," Cassidy confessed. "I could've sworn Blue was hitting on Stephanie, which was going to be very interesting to watch considering... Well, considering

Stephanie. But he honestly went in, showed her where the chocolate was stashed, then left."

"He's a complicated man, our Blue." Jace caught her ankles and lifted her feet into his lap. After undoing her laces, he slipped off her shoes.

"What are you doing? Oh. My. *God.*" Cassidy all but melted into her chair because he'd dragged his thumbs along the sole of her foot and all the little nerve endings there pumped their hands in the air, cheering madly.

"It's been a long day. And you don't want chocolate." Jace said it softly, the sexy low hum in his voice sending other parts of her body into raising their hands and cheering as well.

"Already had chocolate. This is better."

She sounded drunk, but who cared? As long as he kept doing that thing he was doing. Or maybe he should be doing the thing he was doing to more than her feet—

Bad thoughts. Bad thoughts considering she'd just met the man and he was hugely tangled in everything she needed to deal with in the days to come. But even the *idea* of his hands touching more places turned her on.

He chuckled softly. "You just made some amazing faces. What's going on in that head of yours?"

"Far too much, and none of it logical," she complained.

"Why does it have to be logical?"

Good question, considering she was talking to a man who could turn into a wolf and all. "Tell me more about the wolf thing."

Thank goodness the man could multitask. His hands didn't stop moving. "What specifically? It's a pretty big topic."

"What do you call yourself? Are there a lot of you here

in Alberta? I'd assume you'd prefer to live in the country, but I know some of you must live in the city."

He pushed extra hard and interrupted her questions because she was too busy moaning to speak. "Before I have to write a ten-page novel, let me knock those off. We say *wolves*. *Werewolves*, sometimes. *Shifters* definitely works because then you can add a designation of what type. Wolf shifter, cat shifter, cougar, eagle."

"Ah. All predators."

Jace paused. "Not exactly. Nothing that can't hold its own. Like, if you're looking for hamster shifters, it's not happening. And for the life of me, I still have not figured out the physics of the eagles and hawks with their weight-to-mass ratio. I will say, every avian shifter I've ever met has been fucking huge in their animal form and on the short side in their human form but packed with muscles, like walking brick shithouses."

So many questions—she hadn't even thought about the size difference between the two forms.

"How come you know about shifters?" Jace asked.

He was squeezing her toes, and it felt really good and really close to ticklish, which meant she smiled as she answered, "I saw someone shift. It was unexpected but in a situation and setting that I absolutely was not allowed to freak out, so I didn't. But the person didn't know how or why either, so for years, Stephanie and I have known it's possible but not any details."

And that was all she was going to say, at least for now.

A furrow formed between his brows. "You're not telling me something."

"Isn't it a wonderful feeling?" she teased before leaning forward and laying her hand over his. "Sorry. I'm not being mysterious to be annoying. It's not my secret to tell, but I promise to ask for permission to share as soon as possible."

"That works."

He carefully positioned her feet in his lap before leaning back with his hands resting over her arches. Beside them, the fire crackled. Add in the sounds of animals in the bush and the wind shaking the leaves in the trees, and it was like something out of a wilderness movie soundtrack.

So many questions, but she was running out of steam. She met his gaze—those gorgeous, mesmerizing deep blue eyes that seemed to look right into her soul. "I'm going to turn off the rest of the questions for now except for this one. Are you doing something that's making me feel like this?"

His gaze grew hotter. Heavy-lidded. "How are you feeling?"

She went with the truth. "As if I've known you forever. As if every detail I don't know about you is something I desperately want to learn." She let her gaze drift over him. "As if I want to take you to bed and not come up for a week."

Jace swallowed hard. He took a deep breath in, nostrils flaring, eyes closing briefly before he connected with her again. "I solemnly swear I am not doing anything nefarious. But this connection between us? It's because of the wolf thing, and it's real. Every single thing you said you feel, I feel it too."

Well, then. "Okay. Good to know."

They sat in silence for a moment, and then Jace stood. Before she could do anything, he scooped her up in his arms.

"Whoa, there, wolf man," Cassidy began.

"Don't worry. You're exhausted. I simply don't feel like putting your shoes back on." He carried her into the kitchen as if she were weightless before carefully placing her on the floor and then stepping away. "Blue will be back in the morning. I'll set up in one of the cabins, so I'll be here as well. All the rest of the questions can wait."

Cassidy stood there in her bare feet as the wolf shifter she absolutely had the hots for politely dipped his chin and walked out the door.

It was exactly what she'd asked for and exactly what needed to happen. Disappointment still welled up inside, and that said more to her than anything about this wild, mixed-up, amazing day.

8

———————

_J_ace made it as far as the first cabin before frustration and hunger took control. He barely stripped his clothes off before the shift rolled over him. His spine realigned and colours adjusted as he changed from human to wolf with the ease and pleasure of over thirty years.

Under his paws, the earth trembled.

Or maybe that was still him reacting to the outrageous need that swelled inside. Need for his mate threatened to sweep all rational human plans to the curb, and while he had zero problem with winging it sometimes—

He ran. Body lengthening on each stride, he thrust his hind legs back hard to propel himself forward at top speed. He wove in and out of the trees with a seemingly carelessness that was complete trust in his wolf.

Body flying, muscles straining, his thoughts shifted from analytical toward more primal. He welcomed the connection with the cool dirt underfoot and the kiss of nature against his fur. The scent of animals in the bush, the lingering aroma of barbecue from a neighbouring acreage.

And her. Always her, dammit. Cassidy was already in him, and he was thrilled and yet so fucking tangled up inside.

A mate. He had a bloody *mate.*

Blue had said it earlier—having a mate changed everything. Jace might have come back to Timberwolf Lodge reluctantly, but hell if he wasn't going to stay.

Staying meant challenging his cousin Del. Instead of avoiding conflict as he'd worked so hard to do over the years, Jace prepared to do what it took. Anything. Everything. Including an aggressive and potentially deadly change of leadership.

It wouldn't happen without blood. The idea was far less frustrating when he considered it as a wolf.

The strongest leads the pack. I am the strongest— therefore I should lead. ·

The thought was purely wolf, yet his human side had to agree.

Jace slowed his pace. The sureness of the problem and the solution should have felt bigger with dazzling lights and the hallelujah chorus going off in the background. Instead, the realization brought him a quiet inner peace.

Even knowing Del might not survive the confrontation couldn't make Jace and his wolf lose the contentment.

He ran expanding circles around Timberwolf Lodge. Checked the territory markers, added a few of his own. Began to stake a claim on the land the way his auntie wanted.

It was nearly midnight when he circled past the lodge one final time, close enough to see motion on the front porch.

The scent of her had filled his senses the entire evening, but now she was right there. From the shadows of the rickety porch, Cassidy watched without a trace of fear in her green eyes.

He should've turned away. Should've followed his resolve to give her the space and time she needed to comprehend exactly how much her world had changed.

She had no real idea. Not yet. Not until they continued their discussion in the morning and all the mornings to follow.

Screw it. Good intentions meant doing what was right for both her *and* him, and right now that meant closing the distance to the porch steps and hopping up them to stop at her feet.

The walls behind her desperately needed to be sanded and stained. The floorboards underfoot creaked badly enough that he had personally checked that afternoon to make sure the entire building wasn't going to collapse around them.

Cassidy wore a pair of boxer shorts and a formfitting tank top, dainty and yet utterly perfect.

A complete and utter contrast. The lodge, his past. Her, his future.

She lowered herself to his level, head tilted to one side. Her expression made him want to do something wild and outrageous.

"I'm going out on a limb here, but I'm pretty sure you're Jace," she said softly. "Yes?"

It was all sorts of wrong but impossible to stop. He leaned forward far enough to lick from her chin to her hairline before she jerked back with a snort.

"Dude. I gotta say it. Doesn't matter how much I was thinking of kissing you earlier, your tongue is not going in my mouth when you're furry."

Jace circled, brushing against her and soaking in her

scent. When he came around to face her, Cassidy curled her hands around his shoulders and stroked.

He was no fool. He sat his ass down and let her pet him.

And oh God, he didn't want to think about how she knew exactly what to do, but she not only stroked him the right way. She dug her fingers into the itchy spot behind one ear that made him damn near roll belly up.

"You're soft. But I can feel how muscular you are." Cassidy leaned in again and peered into his eyes. "I know this is all normal and typical for you, but it really is mind-blowing to think you're in there."

She yawned. A huge, enormous thing, and while she covered her mouth quickly, it was too late.

Jace yawned back. He gave his head a shake when he was finally done.

A soft laugh escaped Cassidy. "So. Yawns are contagious even between humans and wolves." She tilted her head toward the door. "I'm going to bed. I was looking out the window and wondered if you'd come back to the lodge before you finally called it a night."

She stood, and he brushed against her shins.

Cassidy seemed to consider, then opened the door. "If you want to come in, I wouldn't mind."

Really bad idea.

Jace's wolf had him through the door and headed up the stairs before he could come to his senses. It was only going to make him even more wild to be around her without being with her. Then again, in some ways, this was the best of bad choices.

Maybe his human couldn't have her yet, but his wolf could absolutely sleep at his mate's side.

～

Her heart rate hadn't slowed down yet.

Jeez, what had she been thinking? It was one thing to know Blue had turned into a wolf in front of them, but there had been no guarantee the wolf wandering past Timberwolf Lodge in the middle of the night happened to be the one shifter she really wanted to see.

Then putting her face so close to those razor-sharp teeth—

And yet, it had made perfect sense. Walking downstairs, stepping onto the porch. Just looking at him, she'd known.

She'd *known* it was Jace. To her core.

Now, as she followed the wolf that was Jace up the stairs and into her bedroom, she found herself grinning. This was way better than any Goldilocks story or any version of "Little Red Riding Hood." It was awesome, this fantasy realm where the man she really wanted to jump, sometime soon, showed up in his shifter wolf form and then hopped on her bed.

She paused beside the mattress. The sheets were still turned down from when she'd rushed to the window and then outdoors. She should crawl in, but she hesitated.

"And now I feel awkward. Do you expect to sleep under the covers? Because I don't know how I feel about that, at least in your furry form. And I was watching you and suddenly wondered if you'd turn in a circle three times before you lie down."

Jace hopped off the bed, and for one horrible moment, she thought that she'd offended him so badly he was leaving.

Instead, he nudged her legs hard enough that she toppled to the mattress. She rolled, and by the time she got herself upright, he'd jumped beside her, grinning a wolfish grin.

He batted at her again, gently nudging her toward the pillow she'd used earlier.

"You're very bossy for somebody who can't talk." Cassidy made herself comfortable even as her mind continued to race. "But you can. Talk, I mean. Wolf calls, I suppose, and howling and yips. I've always wanted to know what yips meant. You've got to have more ways to communicate. Oh my God, I have so many questions."

The wolf that was Jace rolled his eyes then settled beside her, resting his chin on her thigh.

"I know. I know, questions tomorrow." She laid a hand on his head before stroking softly over and over. His eyes closed, and a low rumble of satisfaction started deep inside him. Like a generator on standby or a really satisfied cat purring.

She bit back another snicker. Chances were he wouldn't like the cat analogy.

Instead, she decided this was a great opportunity to tell him something. Since he couldn't interrupt her. No human vocal cords and all.

It would be easier to get the words out while she was stroking him.

"This place is really important to me. To Stephanie as well. And her sister and the kids— God, this place is going to be the change they absolutely need. But for me, I feel as if this is my fresh start and my last chance." She scratched a finger between his eyes as he stared directly at her. "When I won the lottery—Timberwolf Lodge—I gave my notice and then burned a bridge or two behind me. I was working in hotel management, but the new owners for the boutique hotel I ran were terrible. When I knew I had an out, I gave them more than a little piece of my mind. Plus, we sold or gave away everything that wouldn't fit in the minivan. Going back to Toronto isn't an option."

The wolf's shoulders lifted as he sighed heavily. His nose bumped her fingers. A moment of sympathy. A touch of concern in his eyes.

"I'm determined to make this work. I think I'm telling you this because whatever's going on between us, it can't get in the way of Timberwolf Lodge becoming a success. Which means when you do get around to telling me and explaining, I want you to know that in spite of me being very ignorant of all the facts, I am fully in. I can pack one hell of a punch if I need to." She lay back and stared at the ceiling. Damn her honesty streak. "The only thing I'm not very good at is toeing the line when the rules don't feel right. I really hope if there are a bunch of hoops to jump through to get the lodge up and running, that they're challenges we can handle together."

Jace patted his head against her hand. When she curled up enough to meet his gaze, he dipped his chin. Firmly, once. Then he closed his eyes and tucked his head against her. Conversation clearly over.

She stared at the ceiling for a while longer. They'd driven across the country. Confirmed shifters were more than a one-time miracle. There was a wolf asleep in her bed. A wolf *shifter* she hoped to convince to turn back into a man tomorrow so she could kiss him silly.

That was a nice thought to fall asleep to, Cassidy decided.

Waking to an empty bed and not even a warm spot where Jace had been curled up wasn't as nice.

She glared out the window and sighed. "Fine. Another day, another adventure."

Cassidy dressed then peered into the room Steph had selected. A mess of clothes lay everywhere, but there was no sign of her friend.

More garments lay scattered down the hallway and stairs like a trail of breadcrumbs.

Cassidy shook her head even as she stooped and gathered the fallout. "Stephanie. You're such a lazy ass. Taking two trips to the washing machine won't kill you."

By the time Cassidy reached the main floor, the pile in her arms was up to eye level, with still no sign of her friend.

"I'm going to make you carry my shit for the next week," Cassidy threatened. "Stephanie. Where the hell are you? Get your ass up here."

No answer from Steph, but a loud clatter rang against the front door. Cassidy growled with frustration before making a precarious transfer of the load to her left arm so she could jerk the door open with her right.

A moose butt appeared, the weight of the beast sending the enormous door crashing against the wall as the huge creature fell into the grand front foyer.

9

———

assidy shouted even as she scrambled back to safety. The laundry in her arms flew toward the ceiling before falling like rain on the moose.

"Did you bellow?" Stephanie stepped through the door from the basement and came face-to-face with the moose. Or at least its butt. "Shoot."

The creature found its feet and now stood in massive moosey splendor in a place no moose had gone before.

Or at least Cassidy hoped moose weren't a common occurrence around the lodge. Bad enough she didn't quite know how to deal with the wolves that would, she suspected, be hanging around Timberwolf Lodge, but moose?

The big beast stood motionless except for his head, which swayed from side to side as he examined her and Stephanie. Which wasn't quite as scary as it should have been considering various articles of Steph's clothes swayed willy-nilly from his massive antlers like risqué Christmas ornaments.

Steph shakily slid one hand into the air to fend off the creature—as if. "Cass? Suggestions?"

Cassidy glanced around for the closest weapon. Where had the broom gone? "Thinking."

"Think faster."

"Speed of light."

"Faster still."

"Tesseract?"

The moose snorted. A big and totally amused sound, and Cassidy paused.

Where had she heard that exact noise recently? She narrowed her gaze, glaring at the beast with suspicion.

When he snapped his head away from her, staring up at the ceiling like a naughty child caught with their hand in the cookie jar, she knew.

Without a doubt, and without fear, she stepped forward and stuck her finger in the moose's face before Steph's underwear had stopped swinging. "You are in trouble, buster."

"Uh, Cass? What're you doing?" Steph asked quietly. "Moose, big. Us, small. *Baaaaad* move, antagonizing the wildlife."

"He's not wildlife," Cassidy insisted. Considered. "Okay, he is sort of wildlife, but not *wild* wildlife. Hey, buddy. I thought we had a deal. You're not supposed to hang out on my porch."

Behind her, a deep masculine chuckle sounded. "Marvin. Scratching your butt on the doorframe again?"

Cassidy whirled, ignoring her bestie and the moose who was now confirmed to be her freeloading resident nudist.

She expected to see Jace, but what she got was an eyeful of oversized *GQ* lawyer type. Military-short dark hair, well-trimmed beard and mustache, and an impeccable suit she knew cost more than her car. The same midnight-blue eyes as Jace, but the expression was a lot more serious and intense.

"This... You... *Marvin?*" In the background, Stephanie was having conniptions.

Cassidy turned back in time to see Steph snatch a pair of shorts from Marvin's right antler.

Somehow the moose managed to look...sheepish.

"Everything under control in here?" That sexy deep voice again.

Drat. Cassidy shook her head even as she turned back to face the stranger in the door. "I'm usually more on the ball than this. Hello. Welcome to Timberwolf Lodge. Can I help you?"

"Maybe."

The lawyer watched with a raised brow as Stephanie jerked her clothes free one piece at a time, dropping them with soft curses in a pile at Marvin's moose feet. Hooves. Whatever.

Cassidy's life was so weird these days.

"We're not open yet," she began, but he lifted a hand to stop her.

"I know. My aunt informed me of her plans before she left. I'm the one who drew up the legal papers for the lottery. We met online when you signed them. Delaney Vezina."

She shook the hand he stretched out to her. "Nice to meet you in person."

He held her fingers a moment longer than he should have, his gaze dropping over her in an assessing way that didn't quite offend. Too much appreciation in his eyes?

When he did let her go, his expression lightened

slightly, lips turning up in an approving smile. "I'm a little surprised Marvin here didn't upset you more."

Voice smooth like decadent chocolate. Good grief, Delaney really was a handsome man.

Wait— *Was* he a man? Or more?

"Marvin was worse in his other form," Stephanie informed Delaney haughtily. She planted her hands on the moose's butt and pushed him toward the door. "Cabin 7, bucko. I see your hairy ass, moose or otherwise, outside our door again, and I will shave you bald. No—I'll wax you. Brazilian everything. *Everywhere.*"

Marvin tilted his head to get his antlers though the doorframe, quickstepping out the door without a word of complaint. Grunt. Whatever.

At the last second, Delaney snatched the final garment off Marvin's antlers. "I am more than surprised by this twist to be honest." He stepped toward Stephanie, offering the lacy bra to her on the palm of his hand like a jewel. "And you are?"

His voice had gone lower. Even deeper and somehow even sexier, and Cassidy enjoyed it despite herself. Damn, these wolves—because he had to be a wolf—needed to find a way to give sexy talking lessons to the rest of the male population.

The sex appeal was wasted on Cassidy's best friend, though. She tugged her bra free and eyed him with curiosity. "I'm Stephanie. One of the other names on the deed."

"Hmmm." His gaze lingered on Steph longer than it had on Cassidy. He took a deep, deep breath, and his eyes widened. "Interesting. Very interesting."

The front door slammed open again—she was going to

need to reinforce the wall behind it if this kept up. "Jeez, guys. It's a door, not a jousting target," Cassidy growled.

"Get away from them," Jace ordered, skidding to a stop face-to-face with Delaney.

~

WHAT A FREAKING NIGHTMARE.

Jace had spent a few minutes longer at Blue's that morning than intended, and now, for some reason, his cousin Del was alone with the ladies.

"This isn't the place," Jace began, but Cassidy caught his arm and jerked. Hard.

When he glanced back, her glare could have cut glass. "My house. Want to step back a bit? Get out of my guest's face?"

"Your guest?" Jace whirled on his cousin. "Why are you here?"

"Started as a courtesy call." Del's expression grew more thoughtful, and his gaze took in the women in a way that pushed too many of Jace's buttons. "Now I'm angling for a cup of coffee and a long heart-to-heart conversation."

"No time for heart-to-hearts," Stephanie informed them. She scooped up a pile of clothes and whirled toward the basement stairs. "Nice to officially meet you, Delaney. Laundry duty calls. You kick ass, Cass. Love you. That's to Cass, by the way."

"Love you, Steph. Keep it sunny-side up."

"Always."

Then they were down to three—him, Cassidy...

And his cousin. Who was not raving or foaming at the mouth as expected at their first reunion. How wonderful.

How odd.

Jace risked taking a half step back. "I can make you coffee," he offered Cassidy. "In fact, let me make you breakfast. It's the least I can do after sleeping in your bed."

There. Perfect. And to make his claim crystal clear to Del, Jace slipped an arm around Cassidy's waist and smiled down at her.

She didn't smile back.

Instead, she jabbed her fingers into his ribs hard enough that he let go. He kept in the *oof* of pain, though. Some rules had to be respected, and showing weakness in front of his cousin was not an option.

"Don't be rude. And don't assume." Cassidy spoke softly, but with Del's wolf hearing, she might as well have shouted. "You act like an ass much longer, and last night, and your wolf, will be the *only* time you're in my bed."

The grin on Del's face was unspeakably annoying.

Fine. Time to pull it together. If Del could act in an unexpected manner, so could Jace.

He still stood within lunging range of the bastard. "So. Heart-to-heart? Any topic in particular?"

"Not with you," Del said smoothly, stepping back like he was dancing. He peeked down the stairs where Stephanie had vanished then focused again on Cassidy. "You arrived yesterday. Anything I can help with?"

"Not so far." Cassidy wrinkled her nose in an adorable way. "I think you just met the fine print in the contract leaving on hoof."

"Ah. Yes. Sorry." Del had the grace to look guilty. Bastard managed to make it look classy, though, and Jace wanted nothing more than to plant his fist in his cousin's smug face.

Cassidy examined him closely, clearly noting Jace's body position with interest. When she lifted a brow, though, Jace grinned like they were having a Sunday in the park.

Another eye roll followed. "Anyway, to make this simpler. Yes, Steph and I know you get furry."

"Shift." Jace and Del said the word with the precise timing of synchronized swimmers at a national event.

Because, really, some things required unity.

Cassidy planted her hands on her hips, but her lips twitched. "Fine. *Shift*. Second, Blue and Jace have offered to help us. Well, Jace must help for legal reasons. I'm sure you agree."

"*What?*" The smooth polish vanished from Del's voice, and raw outrage remained. "What possible legal reasons does he claim—"

"As my caretaker," Cassidy went on firmly, "appointed to Timberwolf Lodge by the previous owner and notarized by your company, Jace needs to be here to fulfill the requirements of the Very Important Papers you oversaw organizing. Unless...you screwed up?"

Jace had wanted to jump the woman before. Now, as Del physically winced, Cassidy elevated in Jace's eyes to a glorious queen above all queens.

It took his cousin only a second to pull himself together, the anger pushed down and redirected.

Jace had no doubt it would arise at a more appropriate moment, probably one involving Jace's skin. Especially when Del smiled and bared his teeth.

"You're very right." Del tilted his head toward the basement stairs. "So. Stephanie. She's delightful. Anything you care to share?"

Out of nowhere, Blue appeared.

More specifically, he appeared from the basement— which should have been impossible because Jace knew damn well there was no way into the space other than the stairs. Plus, he'd left Blue lounging on the front porch of a cabin minutes ago when he'd scented Del and raced in to confront him.

Yet Blue was here, the scent of Stephanie clinging to him as he slouched indolently and faced the badass leader of the Jasper pack.

With zero fear in his eyes, Blue shoved his hands in his pockets. "I'll go first. Steph's awesome."

Del took a deep, slow breath. A low growl started in his belly that cut off instantly when Blue raised a brow and flicked his gaze toward Cassidy.

"Don't get in my way." Del was all charming and courteous again.

"Hell, no," Blue agreed before reaching out and tapping Del on the nose as if they were once again teenagers fooling around by the lake. "But FYI? *She's* not your way."

Jace had seen wolves lose fingers for less. But it seemed when confronted by the pack Omega, even the big bad knew when to say enough.

Del gathered himself then turned to speak to Cassidy. "You know about wolves. I'm glad because that makes some things easier. You'll need to come meet the pack. Living here and all."

"Might be a good idea." Cassidy considered. "Steph and I will talk, and when it works, Blue and Jace can—"

"Jace isn't invited." Del said it like death warmed over. "You'll understand soon."

"More secrets. Goodie," Cassidy offered with a fake perkiness. "I think you should go. We have things to do."

Del considered, then nodded. "I'll email a formal invite for you and Stephanie. And Blue, of course, comes and goes as he pleases." A calculated mischief rolled into Del's eyes. "By the way, Jace. Emma says hi."

"Emma can bite me," Cassidy muttered under her breath, which meant all of them heard it.

Jace risked losing one of his own limbs to slip an arm over Cassidy's shoulders as they stood by the door and watched Del leave.

"Don't let the door hit you on the ass," she muttered. "Suave bastard."

Delightful, Jace thought. What a wonderful day it was turning out to be.

He twisted toward Cassidy with a smile.

Pain flared, sudden and sharp.

She twisted his ear and hauled him forward, fire in her eyes. "Okay, Cujo. You've got some explaining to do, and this time I want it all."

Had he thought her a queen? Goddess. She was a fucking *goddess*, and Jace couldn't wait to worship her the way she deserved.

10

———

Weird mornings aside, Cassidy couldn't complain of being bored since arriving in Jasper. Boredom had been part of her problem back in the day, if she were honest.

Which was why when Jace winked and nodded, she let him go. "Cocky bastard."

"Isn't he just?" Blue agreed heartily, pushing past them toward the kitchen. "I'll make breakfast."

"Thanks for being supportive," Jace grumbled.

Blue hauled supplies onto the counter before glancing back in surprise. "I am being supportive. I meant Del was the bastard, not you."

"I think you're all arrogant jerks," Cassidy snapped, hauling out a kitchen chair and dropping into it too vigorously.

It collapsed under her.

Before she hit the ground, Jace swept her up in his arms and held her close. "Careful, Goldilocks."

"*Grrrr,*" Cassidy offered before sighing. "Thanks for the assist. You can put me down."

Jace buried his nose in the crook of her neck and breathed deeply. "Nope. Not yet."

She should have struggled, should have gut punched him or something, but he was warm and smelled great, and he was doing that purring-rumble thing again, and she melted on the spot.

When he did lower her a moment later, it was a slow, close release. The front of her body tight to his as she slid toward the floor. Heat wrapped around them, his pupils dark and intense.

Her mouth went dry, and other areas went very, very wet.

Jace breathed deep, then groaned, lowering his forehead to hers. "You're killing me, woman."

The softly spoken words caressed her skin and made her shake inside. Their lower bodies connected firmly enough his interest was proved without words.

She'd felt lust before. Acted on impulse and had wild, outrageous fun with a stranger she'd met at a club or gathering. It had never, ever been this level of off-the-charts need and desire. They should—

"Cream and sugar?" Blue's chipper question disrupted a very hot daydream.

Jace closed his eyes and grimaced. "Blue, you suck."

"Noted. Still need to know how to make Cass's coffee."

She uncurled her fingers from where they'd ended up fisted in the front of Jace's T-shirt. Cassidy smoothed the fabric, hands trembling slightly at the thought of all that muscular power right there, available for the taking. "One sugar, no cream."

Jace's gaze followed her. She knew it even though she turned her back and walked to another chair by the table. This one she tested before sitting her ass down.

No matter the physiological roller coaster she was on, it was time to buckle down and get some answers. She placed her hands on the tabletop and considered the best place to start grilling him.

"What did I miss? Did you make me coffee? Are there any of those mini-doughnuts left from yesterday?" Stephanie rolled in, nabbed the mug Blue offered her in one hand and the plate of doughnuts in the other, then twirled to the table and settled beside Cassidy. "So, Marvin's a moose. Didn't have that on my bingo card."

"There are a lot of things not on my bingo card that I get to mark off," Cassidy said dryly.

Blue put another plate on the table. This one was full of grilled cheese sandwich triangles. He reached for one even as he sat across from Stephanie. "It has been an exciting morning, hasn't it?"

Jace flipped around a chair and ignored the food. He folded his arms over the backrest and offered Cassidy a shrug. "Now you've met Del."

"Your cousin. My lawyer." Cassidy paused for a moment to give herself a real chance to think through the rush of emotion swirling in her gut. Then she decided, *Screw it.* Forget about finesse, it was time to barrel straight through. "He's polished, and smart—"

"—and pretty," Stephanie inserted.

Cassidy kept rolling. "Very pretty. Plus, there's some element of power to him that at first made me want to stop and listen. I like him, but the longer we talked, the more he annoyed me."

Jace's lips curled upward into a grin. "I like you."

"Of course you do. I'm very likable." She took a sip of her coffee. "And I don't *dislike* Del, but it's as if there's something off. Something that's out of balance or mixed up."

Jace's poker face didn't change, but Blue looked thoughtful. "That's a really good way to put it, all things considered."

"How about some more details. Because he's obviously a wolf, and the fact all of us are invited to the wolf hoedown except for Jace says there's something going on that I don't understand."

"Del looked at me funny," Stephanie said. "As in weird funny, not *ha- ha* funny. And then this one"—she pointed across the table at Blue—"appears out of nowhere while I'm loading the washing machine. The next second I'm wrapped in a giant hug. Not that I minded terribly, but it's a good thing I don't have phobias about people jumping out of dark corners."

Another interesting point. Cassidy squeezed Stephanie's fingers for a moment before the two of them turned to stare at Jace.

"Long story short? Del is the Alpha of the Jasper pack. His dad, our uncle Paul, used to be in charge, but the man went off the rails. Someone had to take over, and the usual way to do that in a wolf shifter pack is to prove you're the most powerful."

Stephanie wrinkled her nose. "Why do I think you're not talking about arm wrestling?"

Jace's shoulders lifted, fell. "We're human, but we're also wolf. When Uncle Paul became a danger to the pack, someone had to do something. I would've done it, but Del stepped up first. Which meant I had to acknowledge Del as my Alpha, challenge him to take over, or get the hell out."

There was a whole lot unsaid in that summary sentence. Cassidy needed clarity, no matter how outrageous this all was to her on one level. "When you say Del stepped up, does that mean he did something to his dad?"

Across the table, Blue sighed softly. "Uncle Paul got into drugs. They don't mix well with our shifter side, and he became a threat not only to himself but to the pack. Anyone less powerful than him was at risk, so Del did what had to be done."

Jace still hadn't moved.

Cassidy leaned in closer. "And you didn't want to stay here with Del as your Alpha?"

He met her gaze firmly. "I'm stronger than him. My human side can bow and grovel for a certain length of time, but my wolf absolutely would not accept anything but being in charge. Plus, taking on leadership of the pack would have meant abandoning the project I'd been working on for years that was about to become viable. My work required me to travel away from the pack, which is not what an Alpha does."

He still didn't say the final truth, so Cassidy said it for him. "And taking on leadership would've meant you had to kill your cousin Del."

HIS GODDESS WASN'T LETTING him get away with anything. Inside, Jace's wolf rumbled with approval. "Shifters are pretty basic when it comes down to it. The strongest leads. You prove where you stand in the hierarchy. Fighting is a quick and simple way to figure it out."

Stephanie looked shocked, but Cassidy considered, nodding slowly. "If you were going to leave to finish your project anyway, there was no use in going after Del, who had already taken a huge step in order to become Alpha."

Across the table, Stephanie frowned. "But Del was here today, and other than flexing your macho charm muscles at each other, you two seem to get along."

Blue chuckled. "Macho charm. I like it." He grinned at Jace. "Let me see if I remember this correctly. Because *not* becoming Alpha when you potentially *could* be one is as big a thing as becoming one, Jace and Del did have a confrontation. Del issued a bunch of threats, Jace somehow kept his wolf from ripping Del apart, and at the end of the day, Del was leader and Jace was gone."

"But you're supposed to be Alpha. That's why it didn't feel right when Del attempted to order us around," Cassidy suggested.

It was tempting to leave it at that, but Jace really couldn't. "You're about eighty percent. It doesn't feel right for Del to order *you* around because you're also powerful enough to be a pack leader."

"Get out." She blinked rapidly at him. "I'm not a shifter."

Blue flashed two thumbs up. "You said 'shifter.' Go you."

Cassidy tossed him an annoyed look.

Time to head this in a different direction for a moment. "We've got more to talk about, but if we're going to explain in detail how pack dynamics work, can you explain how you know about shifters?"

The women exchanged a quick glance.

Stephanie took a deep breath then dipped her chin once before explaining. "My sister's first husband was in the military. Stacy got pregnant right before he headed off on tour. He didn't come home."

Cassidy looked down as if she were holding something. "I was giving Colt a bath. He was about four months old when suddenly instead of a baby boy, I had a very wet and squirming wolf in my hands. I knew it was him, so I couldn't freak out or anything. Just held him as he played for a while as a wolf and then switched back to being a kid again."

Blue gave a low whistle. "That's one way to find out."

"Got my heart pumping, I can tell you that much," Cassidy agreed.

Stephanie joined in. "We did as much research as we could, but Colt's daddy had no family we knew of. So, the three of us figured it out as we went along. Colt's a great kid, and he's got really good—what would you call it? Control? Stacy was a little worried that heading off to school would be a problem, but he's never once shifted when he's away from home."

"That's impressive," Jace agreed. He lifted his chin toward Blue. "I wonder if he's got any of your tricks up his sleeve."

"Possible. Poor kid, though. It's hard to grow up outside a pack. Wolves do better when they've got others around." Blue frowned. "Stacy has three boys. What about the other two?"

"Human. And their daddy is not in the picture because he turned out to be an asshole." Stephanie pointed at Blue. "Explain the 'tricks' comment. Del is an Alpha—in title at least. And Jace is an Alpha—it's what he is for real and should be for the pack. What are you?"

"Magical." Blue wiggled his fingers.

Stephanie snickered.

Blue pressed a hand to his chest and looked offended. "You wound me. I'm being serious."

"As annoying as it is, I have to back him up," Jace offered. "Blue is one of those rare wolves we call *Omegas*.

They slip through the cracks of power and get away with a lot of bullshit."

"This is backing me up?"

It felt good to poke his cousin. "Blue sometimes knows ahead of time how things will turn out. He still sucks at poker, but if he tells you to jump, he means it."

Cassidy finished her coffee and put the mug back on the table. "Yesterday, when you decided to shift, that's because your Omega superpower told you it was the right thing to do."

Blue nodded.

"Well, that was convenient." Cassidy tilted her head to Stephanie. "Sounds like maybe Colt's wild intuition has an explanation."

Stephanie's expression tightened. "Maybe. Poor kid." She bounced a glance between Jace and Blue. "Will he be welcome in the pack? Because it sounds as if that's something he needs."

"Absolutely. Pack is all about kids—about family and connection. We fuck up other parts of it at times, but at the core, that's what a pack does best."

And Jace was going to do everything he could to make sure all of it worked. Including the area he was still avoiding. The bit about him and Cassidy.

She examined him, suspicion in her eyes. "You really are terrible at full disclosure."

"It's been a short time and a lot of information," he countered.

"So you plan to casually mention I could lead instead of Del and not say anything else? Because that implies at some point, I could be invited to take part in a violent physical challenge, which I'm not really okay with, human frailties and all."

She was right. That was a terrible place to leave this.

Jace glanced at Blue, who simply lifted his shoulders in a noncommittal shrug. "Your call."

Great. No help from that quarter. At least Blue wasn't warning him off.

Only he wasn't doing this here. Jace wrapped his fingers around Cassidy's arm and pulled her to her feet. "Come with me."

She moved with a subtle grace, catching up and marching by his side as they headed through the living room and out the front door.

The morning sunshine was breaking through the trees, and dashes of bright yellow bounced off the rich green grass underfoot. A perfect June day and a perfect moment to examine further.

He came to a stop under the massive white pine at the edge of the forest. The trail they'd run on so many times as children, in both human and wolf form, started at their feet then disappeared into the cool, life-scented woods.

He turned to face Cassidy. Caught her hands in his and pressed her palms to his chest. "Close your eyes."

One of her brows arched upward, but she followed his instructions.

Jace stared at her for a moment, taking in the smooth curve of her cheeks, the dark line of her eyelashes at rest, her face serene and peaceful. A dark-haired beauty standing and trusting him implicitly.

His heart gave a kick, and he wanted to shout and roar and howl in delight.

Instead, he reached out to her with the other part that lived inside him. "Listen. Feel. Learn."

11

They stood with the sun washing over them. A gentle heat brushed her shoulders with a kiss that refreshed and promised a beautiful day.

As Cassidy closed her eyes, her senses sharpened. The birdsong grew brighter, and the springtime scent of green growing things, sharper. Under her hands, Jace's heart pulsed over and over, hard enough that her hands moved in rhythm.

Listen. Feel. Learn.

The words had been spoken with his deep sexy voice but also something other. A wildness sprinkled on top. Something earthy and primal, and while she knew she still stood there, sunlight prickling on her skin, she was moving.

On four feet, low to the ground. Rushing through the trees, darting high, shifting low. Rich scents in her nostrils, blood pounding in her veins.

A wolf. She was—a *wolf.*

Running through the woods, exploring her territory. Feeling the connection with the land under her feet and the air rushing through her fur.

It was astonishing. It was unbelievable, and yet it felt so right.

She stopped. Four feet planted firmly as the brittle rock underneath dug into the pads of her paws. She stood on the ridge of a mountain, looking down over the valley. Timberwolf Lodge sat beside the jewel-bright blue waters of the lake. Her land—*their* land.

Their home.

"How?" Her voice sounded rusty, her throat dry as if she hadn't spoken for years.

"Some humans can connect. You can't physically shift— not ever. There's no virus or anything that will affect your body and make you into a shifter. But you've got wolf in you. You need to learn how to let her out."

Cassidy opened her eyes. She stood where she'd started, on a trail under a massive tree. Her palms remained pressed to Jace's firm chest. He'd wrapped his arms around her shoulders, cradling her to him.

"Is this because of you?" she asked.

He looked reluctant but then answered, "It's because of us. I'm a catalyst, but so are you. Putting us together makes the magic happen."

"Me and any Alpha wolf?"

Admiration flared in his eyes. "You are so damn smart. No."

She thought about everything he'd said, between the conversations this morning and the sensations she'd experienced during the time Del had been there. All those thoughts whirled together as she added everything up. "You're an Alpha. That's what you and Blue said. That you should be Alpha instead of Del."

"And I'm going to be. I need to figure out a way to do it

that doesn't involve having to put Del six feet under. He's not a bad guy, he's just…"

She made a face. "He's in the way."

"Pretty much." He brushed his knuckles over her cheek. "You and I are both here because my auntie decided to shake things up around Timberwolf Lodge. There's a lot we need to accomplish, and every step of the way, you get to make choices. But here's one thing I can guarantee you. I've made my choice, and that's to do what needs to be done. Not only for the pack but for you. I'm in it for the long haul."

A slow tremble rocked his body as if he still held back. So much information, most of it incredible, and yet all of it somehow connected and looped in a way that tangled her up with him.

With Jace.

Cassidy stepped back. It took far too much physical strength to make that small move. "This thing—this incredible thing—it's not going away, is it?"

He shook his head.

She took a deep breath. "Then as much as I want to rush in and experience everything all at the same time, let's slow down. Let's do the next thing because you're right. There's a lot we need to accomplish. I need you to warn me, though. If I'm stepping off the rails when it comes to the pack. To what needs to happen with Del. Because I agree. I'd really prefer for him to not be dead."

"I can work with that," Jace promised.

He gestured toward the house, and they walked back in a companionable silence. Which was good, because her brain was so full, she couldn't fit another thing in.

Jace took off toward the workshop. Cassidy entered the house by herself.

She found Stephanie upstairs setting up the computer. "I thought there was no reception?"

"Blue climbed up on the roof and did something, and now we have satellite, so we have internet." Stephanie wiggled her fingers in the air. "Ta-da. Magic."

"Don't think that's quite the type of magic they were talking about," Cassidy said.

"It's as good as," Stephanie insisted. "Stacy's going to be online in a minute. She's going to lose her mind when she hears about shifters."

It was good news, but her best friend looked concerned.

Cassidy laid a hand on Stephanie's shoulder. "I've got more to tell you as well, but this much I can say; I think... No. I'm *certain* things are going to turn out well."

Less than a minute later, they were huddled around the monitor. On the other side, Stacy waved her fingers. Her hair was pulled back in a ponytail, shadows under her eyes.

"Hey, sis. You hanging in there?" Stephanie rested her chin in her hands. "You look as if one of the kids was up last night."

Stacy nodded then broke off to cover a yawn. "Sorry. Yeah, I got up to check on the kids, and Ace was missing. He had a nightmare and crawled into bed with Colt. When I found them, Colt was—"

Stacy waggled her fingers in the air, not saying it, but they all knew she meant Colt had shifted into a wolf. His little brothers knew. Both Blaze and Ace found it hugely comforting to cuddle with Colt when he was furry.

This was going to be one hell of a chat, Cassidy suddenly realized.

Stacy smiled, patting back some loose hair that had fallen from her ponytail. "They're all fine now and busy watching TV. Tell me about the lodge. Is it going to work? Are we excited?"

Stephanie and Cassidy exchanged glances then glanced back at the screen.

Cass began, "There are a million things to tell you, but yes, it's going to work. Yes, we are very excited."

Stephanie held up a hand. "And a lot of those million things we will have to tell you later, but this needs to happen now. Colt is not the only person who can turn into a wolf."

Her sister frowned. "I assumed he wasn't. But how do you know that for sure?"

"Because Timberwolf Lodge has wolves. We met them. We've seen it." Stephanie hurried on because Stacy's jaw had dropped. "It's okay. It's better than okay because I think this is exactly what Colt needs. There's a pack here—like a family that also can do what he does."

Stacy's expression raced through shock, wonder, excitement—

Stephanie winced. "We told them about Colt."

Her sister's face went white. "Steph. How could you?"

"It was my fault." True or not, Cassidy took the blame. "I know it sounds scary right now, but trust me. Please. You know I love Colt, and I would never do anything to hurt him. This is going to be a good thing. I promise."

Stacy pressed her hands to her cheeks, eyes closed. "I do trust you. I'm scared right now, though. I'm not afraid to say that. I couldn't bear—"

"Nothing's going to happen to him, I swear." After all the wonders Cassidy had experienced over the past hours, it must be true. "We've met good people. And by the time you arrive, we'll have a solid place for you to land. You and the boys." Cassidy said it with conviction and felt it to the pit of her stomach.

Now to make it happen.

~

FOR THE REST of the day, and the two days after that, Jace deliberately kept himself out from underfoot.

There were plenty of things on the to-do list Blue and Stephanie had put together that required grunt labour. Working hard and staying away from Cassidy seemed the only way to give her the time and space she needed to deal with all the changes.

So instead of following her around like a panting puppy, he ripped apart rotting floor boards and bucked up fallen trees into two foot sections. Filled the woodshed. Cleaned out gutters and power washed the outside of the cabins so they could start staining. Dealt with his cousin Pete's truck and arranged to have his own vehicle brought to town.

In the off moments, he connected via satellite to his company and set up for an extended leave. He had people in place so things could keep running even while he was gone. Exactly how a good business should run.

He willingly traded the boardroom for a hammer and nails and couldn't be happier. It was honest work, rewarding work.

Work to make Cassidy happy.

It was amazing to see changes happen quickly in some circumstances. They had a bunch of things on order for the renovations inside the house, but the outside work was something he enjoyed. Cool enough in the morning and evening that he could start early and finish late.

Just before lunch on day three of his self-imposed fast

from Cassidy, Stephanie marched up and thrust forward a large glass of lemonade. "Since you refuse to come to the house, I've been commanded to keep you hydrated."

Jace glanced involuntarily toward the lodge. "Thanks."

"You really don't have to avoid us. Or her. Cassidy told me about the whole 'runs with wolves' thing. It sounded incredible." Steph folded her arms over her chest and waited as Jace tipped back the glass and drained it in one go. When his gaze met hers again, she spoke softly, as if encouraging secret sharing. "Are you keeping away from her because that's uncomfortable? To do that connection thing?"

"I'm avoiding her because what I'd like to do involves naked time with Cassidy, not home repair." He slapped his mouth shut the way he should've before the words escaped.

Stephanie grinned. "See? I *knew* you could come right out and say it. I also know Cassidy would not be opposed to naked time. Just don't do it in the kitchen. I'm still traumatized by Marvin."

She took the empty glass from him and twirled away, marching off with a jaunty whistle.

Jace shook his head. He'd thought Blue was one of a kind, but obviously, he and Stephanie were two peas in a pod.

A day later, Jace pounded in the final nails on the rear roof repair for Cabin 7. Marvin pulled out a lawn chair and strategically arranged it so he could watch the entire event. "You missed a spot."

Jace kept hammering with his right hand as he lifted his left and flipped the bird at the moose shifter.

Marvin sipped his beer and grinned. "You do good work, for a wolf."

"Considering I've never seen you work, I don't know that you have any concept of what the word means."

"I have worked in the past. Manual labour, even. Can't recommend it." Marvin lifted the longneck again and tilted his head to the side. "This place going to get full up with visitors?"

"At some point. That's the plan."

Marvin sighed. "Well, paradise can't stay paradise forever. You tell that mini-Amazon that when she needs some help, I'll pitch in."

"Really?" Jace was shocked enough to stop his task. "What are you going to do? Serve hors d'oeuvres?"

"Childcare." Marvin glared at Jace from under his bushy eyebrows. "And before you think something terrible, I have been vetted by the RCMP and have the paperwork to prove I have no criminal record. Plus, I'm certified as an early childhood development instructor."

Marvin sniffed then leaned back in his chair. He tilted his hat down to cover his face and proceeded to ignore Jace.

Just proved it was nearly impossible to read someone based on appearances.

Jace cleaned up his tools and headed for the cabin he and Blue had appropriated. He didn't bother to shower but went straight to the fridge, pulled out another iced tea, and tipped it back.

He settled in the chair on the porch to stretch his legs and close his eyes for a couple of minutes. Getting up early and staying up late was a great distraction but tiring. Combined with the hard physical labour, Jace had lost any boardroom flab he'd gained living in the mostly human world.

Not to mention his nightly runs through the trees,

although during those, he admitted his wolf seemed a little too eager to hunt.

If I can't sink my teeth into Cassidy, I need something else tasty on a nightly basis.

"You're a mess." The porch boards creaked slightly as Blue took the stairs and crossed to sit in the chair at Jace's side.

"If you can't say something nice..." Jace began.

His cousin snickered, raising his water glass in the air in a mock toast. "My mom was royally pissed when you changed the end of that saying from Disney approved to wonderfully vulgar."

"Hey, 'eat shit and die' is not *that* vulgar," Jace protested.

"You plan to teach it to Stacy's kids?"

Damn. "Point taken." Jace twisted his head to get a better view of Blue. "Where do you get these clothes? Gaudy-AF Outfitters?"

Blue glanced down at his neon-yellow shorts and pale purple T-shirt. "These are school team colours."

"For Puke Academy?" Jace grimaced. "You and I went to the same school, and we did not have those as our school colours."

Blue lifted his nose in the air. "I never said *which* school colours. Anyway, onto a far more important topic than where I find my breathtakingly wonderful apparel—what the fuck are you doing?"

Taken aback, Jace opened both eyes and gave his cousin his full attention. "Did you swear at me?"

"Probably. Most likely. Definitely."

"Death wish?"

Blue snorted. "As if. No, I'm truly curious. Because I understand that I'm following a very particular slow boat to romance and a happily ever after with my mate because that is what the situation calls for. Because I'm insightful and uber-sensitive."

"A real peach." God, his cousin was a kick.

"You, on the other hand," Blue continued, "are not known for great feats of patience, yet you're sitting on your ass and twiddling your thumbs instead of getting on with mating. Which makes me ask, what the ever-loving hell is going on?"

"Patience is a virtue."

"*Procrastination* is a five-syllable word," Blue volleyed back.

Jace caught himself counting then cursed. "Such an ass."

His cousin grinned as he leaned forward in his chair. "I think you should do something about your level of frustration. Because sharing a cabin with you is like being roommates with a honey badger. You suck. You toss, you turn, you stay up all hours of the night."

"You really think I should make a move?" Jace held up a hand. "And not because I'm disrupting your beauty sleep."

"Yes," Blue snapped in a rare show of impatience. The next moment, he leaned back and returned to his carefree slouching. "Not that I've had any ominous premonitions or specific insights, but I think acting sooner than later is going to help you. Can't say exactly why, but please. Go on. Release the Kraken."

Jace kept his expression poker straight. "I had no idea you knew what I'd named my cock."

Water flew from Blue's glass directly into Jace's face as his cousin rose to his feet, shaking his head in amused disgust. "And on that note, I'm headed back to the house. Stephanie and I are removing wallpaper from guest rooms two and three. Won't be around until dinner. Six o'clock in the main house. You're expected. There's stew in the Instant Pot, and Steph made bread this morning."

As his cousin walked away, Jace flashed back to his conversation with Cassidy days earlier when he'd explained that when an Omega told you to jump, you should get both feet in the air as quickly as possible.

Jace went looking for his mate.

12

———

Cranky beyond belief, Cassidy shoved the pitchfork into the ground and loosened another section of weeds. "Sure. Tell me your wolf is all Alpha powerful and then go off and hide for a bloody week."

She snatched up the nearest weed and hurled it into her bucket with far too much vigour. Grumbly thoughts continued to roll through her brain as she slammed the pitchfork into the ground over and over.

Her phone pinged in her back pocket. Blue had gotten an internet connection organized for the entire lodge area, which was a blessing and a curse. She hated being constantly on call, but still, Cassidy pulled it out to make sure it wasn't Stacy needing something as she did her final preparations back in Toronto.

Email from the Jasper pack.

Cassidy Rundle, Stephanie Nix.

Considering the history between the Jasper pack and the

previous owners of Timberwolf Lodge, I felt it best to do this officially.

You are invited to join the pack for the upcoming Sunday picnic. We'll be gathering at the Ridge Fairgrounds starting at two p.m. This is a family-friendly gathering until approximately eight p.m. when it becomes adult only. As our guests you are not expected to bring anything, but the event is a potluck.

We do expect you to honour our no-camera rule. If you need to bring your phone in case of emergency, I will be available to hold it in trust.

There will be children in attendance. I think you can agree that protecting them is our highest priority.

Huckleberry Carter may escort you to and from the fairgrounds.

Looking forward to seeing you both.
Delaney.

Most of her anger vanished in the consideration of the Sunday event. Just the thought of more wolves, more shifters—

The idea made her damn near giddy on behalf of Stacy and Colt.

"That's a happier expression than you were wearing a few minutes ago."

She tilted her head up as she shoved her phone into her back pocket. Jace towered over her for a second before squatting at her side. His jeans were covered with dust, dirt showed in the ridges of his knuckles, and a dark streak was smeared across the bridge of his nose.

Even filthy, he looked delicious, and the thought pissed her off.

Stay cool. Stay even. "Invitation to the Sunday picnic."

"Ah." Jace nodded then adjusted position and began pulling weeds from where she'd loosened the soil. "It's a pretty big deal. It's a good step, considering you now live here and all."

"I'm thinking about Colt," she admitted. "He's such a good kid, but he's always felt different, which, hello. He is. I think this will be good for him."

Jace stayed quiet for a minute, using the pitchfork from a kneeling position and prepping the next section of the flower bed without breaking a sweat. "All kids need to feel they belong. Forget that—*everyone* needs to feel they belong."

He gave a pointed glance in her direction before going back to work.

She rocked back on her heels, knees resting in the freshly turned dirt. "What are you implying?"

He gave a gentle lift of his shoulders. "You said you needed to make this work. Timberwolf Lodge. The whole move to Jasper. That you burned bridges. Sounds as if where you were wasn't where you needed to be."

Nail on the head. And that just pissed her off all over again.

"Where do you get off telling me what I need?" Cassidy demanded. "I'm not saying you're wrong, but I'm saying I don't know if I want to have a conversation with you after you've been who the hell knows where for the past few days. You pull me along on some magical, mystical werewolf carpet ride, and then I can't find you to ask questions. I see you across the yard chopping wood in nothing but your jeans and sexy, sweaty muscles, and I can't sleep at night because every time I close my eyes, all I see is you, and I ache."

Damn it. Cassidy wanted to slam a hand over her mouth, but it was now obviously five miles' worth of words too late.

Jace squatted there beside her, balanced on his heels, a hungry look in his eyes and that cocky grin pasted on his face. Dimples in full force. She couldn't take it anymore. Bastard.

She leaned forward, planted both hands on his chest, and shoved with all her might.

Somehow, between touching his torso and setting him in motion, the entire world rotated. He wasn't flying away from her; she was moving in unison with him, hovering in mid-air for a split second before landing gently on her back with him over her.

Muscular arms were braced on either side of her head. His thighs rested on either side of her knees, pinning her in place from the waist down as he lowered himself until their groins connected.

His chest rocked in and out in an unsteady rhythm. His midnight-blue eyes shimmered with silver. His nostrils flared for a second, and then his eyes closed as he seemed to savour the scent of her.

"That's not what I thought would happen," she confessed, her voice a near whisper. As if she could say or do something and make this vanish. Make it change. And dear God, she might not know what the hell was going on, but she did not want it to stop.

"Cassidy?"

God, his voice. Like a velvet vibrator straight between her legs. "Yes?"

He lowered. Another inch. Lips closer. Gaze fixed straight on hers. "I ache too."

And then he kissed her.

~

This was going way too quickly after having been stalled for way too long. Just touching her, being over her, was enough to make his wolf go wild.

The scent of her filled him, and the knowledge that she'd been craving him just as much made the pain of the past days sweeter.

Wasn't that fucked up?

Jace brought their mouths together, nipping at her lower lip and taking full advantage when she gasped. He swooped in and consumed her. Feasting on her, taking in every gasp and moan and accepting the challenge she gave back just as fast and furious.

The sharp bite of her fingernails into his back shot pleasure along his spine. When she dragged them lower, scratching him, Jace wanted to strip her down right there and take her.

The small touch of civilization that lingered in his brain told him there was a better solution. A second later, he had her off the ground, in his arms, and was bounding into his cabin.

His buttons went flying as Cassidy ripped the shirt open. She shoved it off his shoulders as he lowered her far enough that her feet hit the floor in the bathroom.

"Do you want this? Do you want me?" he demanded

even as he gripped the bottom of her T-shirt and stripped it over her head.

She paused in the middle of opening his jeans to look him straight in the eye. "Yes. I want you."

He grabbed her by the waist and lifted her onto the counter, fingers sliding up to cup her breasts. A moment later, the sports bra blocking her from his touch was shred to ribbons, leaving rose-tipped breasts for his mouth to feast upon, for his tongue to tease.

Cassidy dragged her fingers into his hair and made fists, tugging tight. "More," she demanded.

Her dirty fingers left lines on his biceps. The dirt from his hands left hand-shaped imprints on her breasts. They were definitely going in the shower, but first—

"Grab my shoulders," he ordered. And when she followed the directions, he lifted her just far enough to drag off her shorts and underwear in one smooth move. He dropped her back on the counter, spread her legs, and covered her sex with his mouth.

The taste of her rushed in, igniting his system, making him wild. This was what he'd been waiting for all his life. To be with her, to give to her.

To make her scream his name.

SHE WAS FILTHY, covered with dirt and sweat. So was he. There was a perfectly good shower not even two feet away that they could use, get cleaned up, and go have some mattress sex.

Jace obviously didn't give a damn about doing things the typical way. Instead, he was doing his best to make her lose her mind right where she was. Perched on the edge of the sink, her knees pressed wide as he took control of her pleasure. Every touch, every lick, exactly where she needed, exactly what she wanted.

He focused those mesmerizing blue eyes on hers, slowing the motion of his tongue. The smile on his lips as he teased made her arms quiver as she braced them on the vanity.

"You're going to come for me," he informed her. "And I'm going to lick up every drop. You are so fucking delicious."

Watching his tongue made the sensations that much sharper. That much more intense. Cassidy could close her eyes and make it last longer or keep watching and be poured out over the edge of the cliff in seconds flat.

He looked up again, but this time his expression grew more serious. "Let go, babe. I'll be here to catch you."

Then slow was gone, and he was bringing her up, storming the castle. Driving her so hard and hot and fast that she didn't only ignite, she imploded. Pleasure streaked from her core to the extreme ends of her limbs as her breath hitched, and she moaned out his name.

A second later he had her in the shower, his soapy hands rubbing her from top to bottom. He touched every erogenous zone she'd known she had and invented a few new ones along the way. The dirt from her body and the sweat from his swirled down the drain and away as her sensitive nerve endings danced once again.

He used his fingers now, easing her up. Opening her as he gazed into her face with a kind of awe in his eyes.

She put her hands to his shoulders and attempted to climb him. "Now. *Now, now, now,*" she begged. Thank goodness for birth control because hell if she knew where the nearest condom was.

One motion and her feet came off the ground, and she wrapped her legs around him.

And then he was pressing her to the wall of the shower, his hardness sliding over her clit. Again and again until she was ready to scream.

On the next thrust, he slid home.

A satisfied moan broke from her throat.

He grunted.

She laughed.

He stood there, pinning her to the wall as they looked into each other's eyes, and amusement danced between them. "You ready for this?" he asked.

When she nodded, the wildness returned. Cassidy held on, consumed with the fire he generated. Pumping into her, thrusting deep and hard, and each motion set off a new set of bells and whistles until her entire body was a firecracker ready to explode.

Beside her ear, his panting increased. The firmness of his muscles under her fingers felt like titanium.

Another torrent of pleasure unleashed itself, and Cassidy called out. His name? The hallelujah chorus? She was too busy enjoying the orgasm to know. Enjoying how his rhythm broke and Jace swore, stopping deep in her as her pulsing pleasure wrapped around him.

He stood there, supporting her, as the shower rained down on them. Breathing uneven, chests rocking, bodies pulsing with blood and energy.

Cassidy cupped his face in her hands then leaned in and kissed him. Still connected intimately, the slickness of his body and hers was an erotic contrast with the sweet press of their mouths.

Five minutes later—more?—she lowered her feet to the ground, and Jace soaped up his hands and washed her again. Gentle this time, the brush of his hands followed by kisses until she was ready to swoon from light-headedness.

He dried her off, brought her to his bed, then wrapped himself around her.

"We're going to miss supper," Cassidy warned.

"No. We'll make it. But we have time for this." He pressed a kiss to her temple. "Rest. Everything else can wait."

She savoured the lingering sensations. Pleasure and satisfaction were much better than brooding alone.

Cassidy pressed her face to the crook of Jace's neck and closed her eyes.

13

———

Sitting at the dinner table an hour and a half later, Jace knew he was being an ass to his cousin, but he really didn't care.

Stephanie might not know yet what he and Cassidy had gotten up to that afternoon, but Blue absolutely did. And while he might've given Jace the nudge to make a move, it still had to be like pouring lemon on a paper cut considering the slow-and-no-go plan Blue was currently engaged in.

Smirking? Absolutely, Jace was smirking.

"More buns?" He held the basket in front of Cassidy. "You've got to keep your strength up."

She glanced at him from under her lids, then rolled her eyes. But she took a bun before resuming her conversation with Stephanie. "You talked to Stacy this afternoon? How's she doing?"

"She's up to her eyeballs in packing, so she propped her phone up on the dresser in the kids' room. I got to encourage Thing Two and Thing Three to get most of their extra clothes shoved into boxes."

"Which meant you spent a lot of time singing the cleanup song," Cassidy guessed.

Blue's eyes lit up. "Oh. I like that song."

"Me too," Stephanie said enthusiastically.

She and Blue both took deep breaths—

"If the two of you start singing at the dinner table, I swear I will find something you don't like to eat and serve it three times tomorrow," Cassidy warned. "And every day for a week afterward."

Blue waved a hand. "Idle threat. I like everything."

Stephanie, though, developed a sudden interest in the ceiling. "Well, now. Maybe we should talk about what happens at the picnic."

A frown on his face, Blue adjusted position until he made eye contact with Cassidy.

She grinned back, almost feral. "Steph has a few things on her hit list that I can pull out to cause good behaviour."

"You're so mean," Stephanie complained before leaning forward, all teasing gone. "But I'm serious. The picnic?"

It wasn't his favourite idea. Jace understood the ladies needed to figure out the pack and where Timberwolf Lodge would fit in. But with the balance of power still out of whack between him and Del, there were too many variables for him to be comfortable.

"The picnic will be a picnic," Jace said as calmly as possible. "They're good people, most of them. And Del won't let anything happen to you."

Cassidy lifted a brow. "That compliment sounded as if someone were pulling your teeth."

"It's that balance thing," he told her. "Del's not a bad person. But he's not where he's supposed to be, according to my wolf."

Blue pushed back his empty plate and met Jace's gaze

straight on. "I'll be with them. I promise, nothing's going to happen on my watch."

"Huckleberry." Stephanie's smile flashed bright.

Jace's cousin waggled his brows. "Sweet enough to eat."

The gagging instinct was too fast to ignore. "Gah. Please. I'm trying to keep my food down," Jace complained.

The rest of the evening passed quickly between dinner cleanup, a few final tasks, and gathering by the fire to make plans for the next day.

Jace found Cassidy's gaze lingering on him, and he took the time to come in close whenever possible. To stroke a hand down her arm. Slide it over her shoulders and squeeze because touching her felt right.

Blue and Stephanie sat to one side of the fire, intently discussing what they wanted to bring to the potluck. Cassidy lowered her voice and tilted her head to the side as she spoke quietly to Jace. "Are you really okay with us going to this thing?"

He blinked. "You said it—it's pretty important not only for the connections to Timberwolf Lodge but for your friend's son."

Her gaze stayed steady on his. "It is important. But you and I seem to be starting something as well, and I want you to know I'm aware you're choosing to let this ride. I might not understand everything within the wolf community, but it feels like a pretty big give to let us go when you're not allowed to be there. And I appreciate it."

His goddess was smart, intuitive, and so fucking sexy, he was going to lose his cool. He leaned in close and brushed a gentle kiss to her cheek. "The fact you shared that with me means a lot. Yeah, I'm fighting some cave-wolf instincts right now, but I'm also interested in your take on the pack."

"As an outside human observer?"

Oh, the innocence of her question. Before very long, she would be leading the pack at his side. Guiding them in all the ways he wasn't able to, their skills lined up for the good of everyone.

What a thrill it would be to finally reach that moment.

He met her gaze steadily. "You're more than human. Remember that. See what you think is right and wrong. What needs to go forward, what needs to change."

She nodded thoughtfully. "I planned to do a lot of assessing, even without your prompting." She fixed her sexy smile on him again. "I had fun this afternoon."

"So did I."

She laid a hand on his thigh and squeezed lightly. "I'm going to hit the sack now. Alone."

She wasn't ready to jump in with both feet full-time, and he understood. He wasn't ready either. "Sleep well."

She vanished into the house, Stephanie following soon after.

He and Blue stretched out their legs and stared into the crackling fire. A quiet settled over them as the coals glowed brilliant red and the logs slowly faded to ash.

"Good day?" Blue asked.

"Good day," Jace agreed. He grinned at his cousin. "Jasper pack isn't going to know what hit them."

"Just control yourself, and don't start a war while we're at the picnic," Blue warned.

Jace snorted. "Please. I have some self-control."

Blue gave him *the look*.

That's all he did, but it was very clearly one step shy of blowing a raspberry. And all Jace could think was, *Yeah, my cousin knows me pretty damn well.*

Especially when Sunday, just after lunch, as Blue and the girls got into the SUV and headed off to the picnic. Jace stood in the roadway and waved until the vehicle took off over the hill.

Not even ten seconds later, he was out of his clothes and shifted into his wolf, taking to the trees.

His mate going somewhere without him? Not happening. It wasn't that he didn't trust her, or that he didn't trust Blue. He just wanted to see for himself that everything was okay.

Yeah. Absolutely no self-control, but so be it.

Jace ran.

~

IT WAS SIMPLY A PICNIC, Cassidy decided, slightly disappointed. Well, a picnic with a lot more canine types in attendance.

Laughing children in both human and wolf form raced everywhere, playing underfoot as adults stood in small circles and caught up. There were teenagers making eyes at each other at the edge of the gathering and interested adults keeping a chaperoning eye on them. There were tables covered with food—

Okay, there were twice as many tables and three times as much food as she'd ever seen at a human picnic, but hey, healthy appetites probably meant a healthy pack.

"You guys okay if I act as guide?" Blue asked.

"You plan to introduce us to the best people," Stephanie guessed. "Which is fine with me, but I'd also really like to know if there are any teachers here. Stacy wanted me to check them out for her. Prep for next year, that kind of thing."

"Sure." Blue glanced around the gathering, swaying

slightly as he waved back at curious onlookers. "You can expect to be overrun by the WMA in short order."

Cassidy raised a brow. "I don't know what that means."

"Wolf Mom Association," Blue explained. "Kind of like PTA but a lot scarier. You have nothing to worry about, but they will go into protective mode first and think later."

"As moms do." Stephanie shrugged. "I don't think you've actually gone to a PTA meeting, or you would not be tossing around words like *scarier*. Honestly, a Karen or a Chad on a rampage can be impressive. Nauseating but impressive."

And then, with all eyes on them, Del walked forward.

Cassidy had to admit he looked just as good in stonewashed jeans and a plain blue T-shirt that matched his eyes as he had in the expensive suit.

He held out his hand to her. "Glad you could make it."

She shook his hand firmly then pointedly glanced around the area. "You've got quite the group here."

"The pack is growing." He turned his attention on Stephanie, and once again there was that next-level attention thing that made Cassidy uncomfortable. "Hello, Stephanie. I wondered if I could—"

Blue stepped forward, his torso knocking Del's hand aside. "Hey, boss. You said you wanted to take care of these." He held up the cell phones he'd taken from them before leaving the parking lot.

"Fine."

The instant Del took the phones, Blue rotated on his heel, wrapped an arm around Stephanie's shoulders, and marched her toward the nearest group of women. "Cassidy. You should come too. Jamie has kids about the same ages as Stacy's. You might want to say hello."

"I'll be right there," Cassidy promised.

Del's gaze drifted after Stephanie, intent enough that this time, Cassidy positioned her body to cut off his view. "Is there something going on I should be aware of?" Cassidy asked.

Del blinked as if surprised to find her there. "What? Oh, it's just that she seems familiar."

"Ever been to Toronto?"

He blinked again. "No."

"Then you've never met her." Cassidy folded her arms over her chest, looking around the group and checking over her shoulder to make sure Stephanie was okay.

As promised, Blue kept close to her side. Meanwhile, Stephanie was being Stephanie, charming the pants off the group of women around her who were all laughing and sharing easily.

Across from Cassidy, the Alpha of the pack took a deep breath. This time his eyes widened, and he examined her more sharply. "Damn. The bastard works fast."

"Come again?"

The crease between Del's brows deepened as he straightened, looking less the businessman and more the wild wolf. "Jace. I can smell him on you."

Oh. *Ugh.* "And that's not the kind of conversation I'm really interested in. Privacy—it's a really good concept."

His lips twitched, and a bit of the suave lawyer returned. "It's also not a concept we're very good at as shifters. I guess he didn't warn you that everyone here would know the two of you fucked."

Temper flares were never a good thing. Cassidy knew it, but her fist still jabbed out before her brain engaged.

Del moved to block her, but she'd shot low and hard.

The next second, he doubled over, cupping his balls. "*Shit.*"

She laid a hand on his back and patted. "I'm so sorry. I really didn't mean to do that. Well, I did mean to do it because you were awfully rude, but I shouldn't have done it, just like you shouldn't have been rude."

Del straightened, a reddish tinge to the blue of his eyes. "You are amazing."

Not the reaction she'd expected. "Thank you?"

He winced and then wiggled his hips for a second before gesturing her toward a nearby table and chairs. "Sit with me and let me apologize."

Cassidy glanced over her shoulder. Blue gave her a thumbs-up and a wink, which either meant he hadn't seen what she'd done, or if he *had* seen, he totally approved. Either way she waved back, then joined Del at the table.

Del examined her for a moment then dipped his chin. "You're the type who appreciates plain speaking, yes?"

"Absolutely."

His gaze floated over her then drifted to where Stephanie was. "You've changed the dynamics. You're strong, and wolves appreciate power. It's very attractive."

Which would explain the initial eye fucking she'd felt from him. "What's up with your obsession with Stephanie, though? Why do you think you know her?"

"Wolf shifters have mates. Lucky wolves have *fated* mates—a level of connection that makes them more than a couple. It connects them on an inner level and makes a pairing something spectacular."

"It's like wolf marriage?"

"But better. When I saw you, I considered making a play because two powerful wolves make a great team." He glanced at Stephanie and took a deep breath as if trying to inhale her scent even from a distance. "She's not powerful, but she smells right. She smells *nearly* right. I'm trying to figure out if she's my fated mate."

"And if she is? Does that mean you plan to grab her and haul her off to your cave?"

This time he looked absolutely horrified. "Please. We're shifters, not obsessive, uncivilized humans. Mating is still a choice for both parties. Being fated mates means we'll be drawn together on one level, but I'll still want to woo and win my partner."

Thank goodness. Because for a second, hearing about fated mates and thinking of the strange draw she had to Jace, Cassidy wondered if she'd already hopped down the bunny trail and swallowed the red pill.

"So having sex isn't enough?" she asked. "To make two shifters permanent mates?"

Del stretched out his legs, grimaced for second, then sighed deeply. "It's not about the sex. You can be mates without sex at all—although mating is supposed to make that better as well. Mating is a choice. Acceptance at a heart level, and mind, and soul."

"That's pretty woo-woo," Cassidy complained.

He grinned. "We're shifters. There's a lot of woo-woo involved in the fact we even exist, don't you think?"

"Definitely." Cassidy nodded. "Thanks for taking the time to clear that up."

"This is as good a place as any to learn about shifters. Since you'll be part of the community. Timberwolf Lodge and all." Del glanced to the side and caught a laughing child as she threw herself at him. He swung the little girl overhead, and she *poofed*. Suddenly, instead of a toddler in a pink sundress, Del held a squirming wolf.

Cassidy's heart raced, but all Del did was laugh approvingly, lowering the little one until he tapped noses with her. "Very well done," he praised her even as he wiggled the squirmy creature out of the pink fabric. "Now where's your mama?"

"Sorry, Del. Didn't mean to interrupt." The young woman stretched her arms out to the child. "Come here, Dixie-girl. Your Alpha is talking to somebody."

"It's never an interruption," Del insisted. He handed the child over to her mother then gestured to Cassidy. "Sophie, meet Cassidy. She's going to be reopening Timberwolf Lodge."

"Oh, that's exciting news." The wolf in her arms exploded back into a squealing little girl. Sophie adjusted the little girl to rest on her hip. "It's been so long since we were out there. Auntie Rachel used to host the best swimming parties."

"You're welcome to come anytime," Cassidy offered. Ideas whirling, she smiled at Del. "In fact, the whole pack is invited. How about Wednesday night? We obviously don't have everything ready at the lodge, but the lake is there, and there's plenty of room to run."

"I like 'wimming," Dixie declared.

"It sounds wonderful. Thank you." Sophie dipped her chin and smiled at them both before moving with her little girl to one side and redressing her.

Cassidy watched for a moment and turned back to notice Del watching her intently. "Is that okay? That the pack comes out to the lake?"

Del nodded slowly. "I'm busy on Wednesday, though. Please accept my regrets."

Oh. "You're not busy. You don't want to come if Jace is there."

He tilted his chin. "As I said, powerful and smart. You're nearly my perfect woman."

"What would make someone perfect?"

Del followed her as they rose to their feet. He took her hand and bent over it before pressing a kiss to her knuckles. "Powerful, smart, beautiful—they're all wonderful traits, but the key component that would make a woman perfect is that she's meant to be mine. Because that means I'm meant to be perfectly hers."

"That's sweet." Cassidy laughed as he made a face. "But it is. And you know? I hope you find her someday. I just doubt very much that it's Stephanie that you're looking for."

He glanced into the nearby bushes, rolled his eyes, then let her hand go. "Enjoy the rest of the picnic. I'll see you soon."

He walked away and rejoined a part of the pack. A tall solid man with haunted eyes and a romantic heart.

Cassidy waited until he was well gone before turning and stepping into the trees. She walked straight up to where Jace waited in his wolf form.

She knelt and wrapped her arms around his shoulders, pressing her forehead to his wolf. "I have no idea how I knew you were here, but I did."

He licked her cheek, and she laughed, turning her face away as she dug her fingers into his fur and scratched all the spots she knew he liked. This whole wolf thing was very strange, but something about it felt like coming home.

Were she and Jace fated mates? Who knew.

Right here, right now was all Cassidy could worry about.

14

———————

"Hand me another board." Blue reached back without looking, and Jace put the material in his hand.

"You do good work," he admitted to his cousin as he admired the ruler-straight edges of the new dock boards.

Blue reached back again, and they fell into a rhythm, inching forward over the newly built trusses Blue had put in place that morning. "It's fun to do something other than furniture," he said. "Not what I expected to be building this summer, but it feels good."

It did, Jace agreed. Once again, his gaze drifted out to find Cassidy where she was working. Unexpected changes, but they felt so right.

There was nothing more to do inside the lodge until their building supplies arrived. And with Cassidy's invitation for the pack to come swimming at the lake less than twenty-four hours away, the girls had revamped the to-do lists into making the outdoor spaces as welcoming and safe as possible.

Thus the work on the dock and the playground Cassidy

had ordered Jace all over the day before. Sanding rough spots and screwing in extra supports and making sure it was as wolf-child resistant as possible.

He and Blue had also spent time on a secret project, and all of it felt like positive forward motion.

Cassidy and Steph were planting flowers in the raised beds surrounding one side of the firepit. Jace had discouraged them from planting anything delicate anywhere enthusiastic little wolves might trample them.

Even now, Cassidy moved with an efficiency that made him grin. He wanted to stroll over, scoop her up, and find somewhere private.

"You are so gone."

He glanced up to discover Blue giving him a super-smirky smile. "You do realize I'm bigger than you."

"Just making an observation." Blue put aside his hammer then glanced at the finished boards under their feet. "Well done, if I do say so myself."

"Your problem is not your building skills."

"I have problems?" Blue pressed a finger to his cheek and considered. "Nope, don't think I do."

"Don't tempt me." Jace glanced back at the ladies again, unable to stop himself.

"I'm not the one tempting you," Blue pointed out. He adjusted his position to stand at Jace's side. "We need to do some planning. The pack coming here for a swim is a good thing. It lets everybody know Cassidy is supposed to be part of this. But you can't hold off on challenging Del forever."

"I know."

Not only because it was wrong to keep Timberwolf Lodge and Cassidy in limbo but because Jace's wolf was running low on tolerance. That balance needed to be adjusted, and soon.

"I think you should enjoy the party." Blue said it like a statement of fact, and Jace gave him his full attention. "Just a hunch, but I think Wednesday is going to be important."

Thank goodness for Omega super senses. "My wolf will appreciate being around the pack again. I've missed everybody," Jace admitted.

"Of course you have. You're a wolf. I know you're not always the smartest wolf, but there's even a place for brawny, powerful, lovable knuckleheads like you."

Jace eyed his cousin. "Don't know that I missed you that much, now that I think of it."

Blue grinned, but then his expression grew serious. "I know there's unfinished business between you and Del because of the Alpha thing, but what the hell's going on with the way he's acting toward the ladies?"

Jace had given it some thought. "Cassidy is powerful. Any Alpha-strength wolf will be attracted to that. Stephanie? I don't know, but he's definitely sniffing after her."

"He sniffs any closer and I'll plant my fist in his nose." Blue picked up his hammer and spun it, balancing the ungainly object on one fingertip like a basketball player spinning a ball.

"Did I just hear my pacifist Omega cousin threaten the Alpha of the pack?"

Blue adjusted his grip on the hammer and glanced down his nose at Jace. "No wolf is truly a pacifist. And we're talking about my mate, even if I'm not staking a claim right now. If Del makes one wrong move?"

He whirled like a streak of lightning, twisting on the spot, arm hurling forward. The hammer flew from his fingers, rotating over and over until it landed with a *clunk*, the claw end embedded an inch deep into the Adirondack chair by the fire.

Jace's wolf heartily approved of the bloodthirsty sentiment. "I'll be right there beside you if necessary."

Blue pushed himself to vertical and gestured toward the land. "After you, Alpha."

Jace paused at the chair to remove the hammer. It took a bit of wiggling to get it out, it had dug in so deep. Yep, it was always good to have people you knew and trusted on your side.

He stopped beside Cassidy. "Looking good."

She stood, making everything inside him grow warm as she casually slipped an arm around his waist to step back and admire their handiwork. "I like the pop of colour. But thank you for the reminder that there may be a few more feet on the ground than I expected."

Jace dropped his arm around her shoulders as they stood there, savouring the connection all the more because she had initiated it. "It's going to be a good party. Thanks for inviting me."

She twisted before pulling herself against him and wrapping her arms around his torso. "Del arranged it so he won't be here. But that doesn't make the problem go away, does it?"

He shook his head. "Blue was reminding me that there'll be a moment of reckoning fairly soon. But not today. Not tomorrow. So let's enjoy getting to know the pack a little better and letting Timberwolf Lodge see some action again."

~

Wednesday dawned beautiful and clear. A perfect June day.

Cassidy stared out her bedroom window at the bright green forest and brilliant sunshine, wondering at the sensation welling up inside her.

Anticipation? Maybe something bigger, as if she were a flower poking its head up through the sun-warmed soil and about to bloom.

Stephanie shoved open the bedroom door and stuck her head in. "It's party day, chica. I'll make the waffles; you make the coffee."

It felt very right to have the four of them in the kitchen, bustling about and making breakfast. It was odd to think it had been barely two weeks since they'd arrived at the lodge, but in that time, Stephanie and Blue had fallen into an amusing routine, chattering like magpies the entire time they worked to make breakfast.

Blue was frying up bacon—a very serious occupation, Cassidy had learned, which involved multiple cast-iron pans and about five pounds of pig. Stephanie had stacks of waffles building on the side counter.

As ordered, Cassidy took care of the coffee because it turned out she was the only one who could make the ancient coffee maker behave.

And Jace—

She paused and took a closer look at what he was doing. "Are those strawberries?"

It was a pile of the smallest red fruit she'd ever seen. But from the sound of approval from Blue, it appeared her guess was right.

"Damn, you found a lot." Blue nodded with approval and then got a glint in his eyes.

"Don't even think about trying to find my secret patch,"

Jace warned. He worked busily, removing the tiniest little green caps. He paused and took one of the berries that was no bigger than a pinky fingernail. "Come here."

Cassidy stepped forward, hand outstretched. He shook his head then closed the distance between them, pressing a hand to her lower back and holding her tight to him as he lifted the strawberry to her lips. "Open up."

As the berry fell on her tongue, she closed her lips around his finger and licked the sweet juice clean. His pupils dilated, and a flash of heat rolled through her even as the flavour burst in her mouth. "Oh. My. God."

Jace's gaze dropped to her lips. "Wild strawberries. Everything wild is just that much better."

Like her wild wolf? Cassidy wanted another taste.

They hadn't had a repeat of their incredible sexual escapade, and in some ways, it felt right not to rush in again. But that craving was there, and their connection and the entire conversation she'd had with Del kept repeating in her head.

Were she and Jace mates? What about the whole wolf connection? How was she to know if this was the right thing, and how did it all fit with the pack?

The questions followed her after breakfast and into the day as they finished preparations for their guests.

Pack members began arriving around eleven o'clock. Families carrying picnic coolers made their way down to the sandy lakeshore. Welcome shouts rang out and hearty handshakes were given as Jace introduced people to Cassidy and Stephanie.

Nearly everyone gave Cassidy a hard once-over. She didn't feel as if it were judgmental or she was being found lacking. More like a healthy curiosity followed by a dollop of approval.

It was always nice to have people nod their head as opposed to feeling the pressure and lack of respect she used to face at her old job.

And there was something very special about the moment when a sweet little girl came racing up and wrapped her arms around Cassidy's knee.

"Well, hello there." Cassidy leaned down to ruffle Dixie's hair. "I remember you."

Dixie let go and raised her hands in the air. "Up," she commanded regally.

Cassidy gathered the little girl up and held her easily. "Where's your mama?" she asked.

The girl's head rested on Cassidy's chest as Dixie popped her thumb in her mouth. A little one-shoulder shrug followed, but then she pointed back toward the edge of the beach. "Silly people."

It only took a moment to spot Sophie. Cassidy moved in her direction and then realized there were a couple of women blocking Sophie in. Hands waved, and their angry tones of voice carried, and Cassidy detoured toward Stephanie.

Her friend looked up from where she was chatting with an older couple who had brought beach chairs and were applying a thick layer of sunscreen. "What's up?"

Cassidy tilted her head to one side. "This is Dixie. Dixie, this is my bestie, Steph. Can you give her a cuddle? I need to do something."

Like the sweet little thing she was, Dixie held her arms out. "Cuddle Steph."

Stephanie snuggled her in and rubbed noses with the little girl. She only made a little noise when Dixie suddenly shifted into a wolf wearing a swimsuit. "Okey-dokey, let's get you untangled." Stephanie glanced at Cassidy. "You okay?"

"I will be," Cassidy assured her. She scratched Dixie on the head. "You be a good girl for Stephanie. I'll be right back."

A straight-line march toward Sophie allowed Cassidy to overhear a few choice words. As she'd suspected, the two women were harassing Sophie.

"Did you really think we wouldn't find out?"

"You should know better than to try to rise above your station."

Oh, how delightful, Cassidy thought. One of the bitches was Emma.

Straight-on attack or sweep their feet out from under them? What a delicious choice.

Cassidy went for the kill. "Hi, Sophie. I'm so glad you're here."

She stopped beside the other woman and wrapped an arm around her shoulders as if they were best friends forever. She glanced at the other two women and sniffed the air. "Oh. Sorry. Didn't see you there."

Beside her, Sophie swayed slightly then straightened her shoulders. "Hi, Cassidy. Dixie and I were very excited to come visit."

"Dixie already said hello. She's with my friend," Cassidy assured her before eyeing the other two women with distaste. "Emma, I know. And you are?"

"Don't even think—" Emma started.

Cassidy held up a hand. "You need to listen better. First, I wasn't talking to you. Second, there's not much you have to say that I want to hear." She looked at the other woman and all but demanded an answer. "Your name."

"Jessica."

Both Jessica and Emma instinctively stepped back as Cassidy moved forward. "Jessica. Emma. I invited the pack to a fun event today, and I assume, as pack members, you want to be included. But if you can't behave, I will rescind your invitation and you can leave."

Emma snorted. "You and what army are going to make that happen?"

Oh, the woman had such a short memory. Ignoring both Jessica and Emma, Cassidy turned her back on them and faced Sophie. "Tell me if I'm wrong, but were these two harassing you?"

Sophie straightened her shoulders again. "They were. It's partly my fault because I need to learn to stand up for myself."

"Well, standing up for yourself is a good thing, but if people weren't jerks, you wouldn't have to," Cassidy pointed out.

Behind her, Emma took the opening Cassidy had left. She laid a hand on Cassidy's shoulder.

It was a simple matter of sliding back one arm, adjusting her balance, and using her hip. Emma flew before smacking on the ground, gasping for breath.

This time Cassidy stepped on Emma's wrist to pin her in place. Then Cassidy glanced at Jessica. "Your choice. Pick better friends to hang out with, or get the hell off my property."

The other woman ran. Right across the beach and into a different group of pack mates.

A prickling sensation at the back of Cassidy's neck made her glance in the opposite direction. A warm glow lit inside her as Jace and Blue wandered toward her.

"Hey, guys," Cassidy said in greeting. Emma squirmed,

but Cassidy only stepped down a little heavier. "Is this something you're supposed to deal with?"

Jace stopped and looked down at the woman on the ground glaring daggers at them. "You look as if you're dealing with it just fine."

"I wanted to make sure I don't cross any lines if I kick Emma out."

Blue stepped in and offered Sophie a hug. "You okay, sugar?"

She nodded. She squeezed him back and then smiled at Jace. "Congratulations."

He held up a hand then gave a little cough. "Nothing to say about that yet."

"But there will be. I know it." Sophie stepped over Emma and gave Cassidy a hug. "Thank you. Oh, and Dixie wants to swim with you later if that works."

"I look forward to it." As strange as it seemed, it also felt immensely right. Cassidy pressed a kiss to Sophie's temple then sent her off toward where Stephanie was building a sandcastle while an enthusiastic little wolf pounced on the turrets.

Meanwhile, Blue had lifted Emma to her feet and now stood beside her like a lazy yet alert watchdog. "Come on, Emma. I'll walk you to your car."

For a moment it seemed Emma would argue.

"Oh, please tell me you want to debate this a little longer," Cassidy said. "I would get so much pleasure out of explaining to you that's not how it's going to shake down."

A flash of anger lit Emma's eyes. But she dipped her chin and looked down, nodding. "I'm sorry for my behaviour."

She turned on her heel and left, Blue sauntering after her.

Cassidy watched her go. "That was weird."

"That was being pack," Jace pointed out.

"She's not really sorry."

"Absolutely not."

"She's going to make more trouble."

Jace grinned and held out a hand. "Won't that be fun?"

And as he led her down the beach toward where a game of volleyball had begun, Cassidy realized he was right.

She *was* looking forward to giving Emma the smackdown she deserved. What a bizarre and yet absolutely perfect thing to anticipate.

Timberwolf Lodge was turning out to be a very entertaining experience.

15

———————

Jace had missed this. So much more than he'd imagined.

Surrounded by pack members, the scent of barbecued hamburgers and hot dogs lingering on the air, the rush of voices and laughter everywhere—he'd *missed* it.

While he'd been gone, he'd had chances to be around other wolves, but it hadn't been home. They hadn't been *his* wolves.

Today was a day for fun, but sometime very soon he and Del would have to face off and make it official because Jace was not giving this up. Not the chance to be a leader to a pack, and not the chance to lead with Cassidy.

He'd been woolgathering, Jace realized, standing at the end of the dock. It was a great place to observe the big picture but frankly a dangerous place to remain motionless without staying vigilant.

A fact he was reminded of abruptly as a pair of teenagers rushed him from the opposite side of the dock.

For a second, Jace teetered with one foot on the wooden

surface, one in midair, then the three of them splashed into the lake like a multilegged cannonball.

The kids surfaced with shouts of delight.

"We rock." Cora held a hand in the air, and Danny high-fived her.

Jace flipped his hair back out of his eyes, grinning with delight at their bravery. "Brats."

"Yes," Danny agreed, ducking under the spray of water Jace shot at him.

Up on the shore, Cassidy's gaze brightened as it met his. Jace stared back, delighted at how much joy she was putting out into the universe simply being with the pack.

In the shallowest part of the lake, the youngest kids were crawling all over Marvin. Blue was helping supervise and lift kids up because Marvin was in his moose form. Children swarmed up his legs, then slid off his back into the water with shrieks of delight.

Little Dixie jumped up and down like a cricket below Marvin's head, reaching up until she snagged her fingers in his bell, the beard-like skin under his moose chin. Jace tensed, but Blue was there, just in case.

Nothing needed. Marvin lowered his head as Dixie demanded, then stood absolutely still as the little girl scrambled up. She stepped carelessly on his nose and then between his eyes, pivoting to land behind his antlers.

She raised her little hands in the air and wiggled enthusiastically. "Giddyap."

Jace and Cassidy exchanged amused glances again, and something else struck him hard and fast.

Being with Cassidy? Absolutely happening. Leading the pack? Sooner than later. Kids sometime in the future? He wasn't ready yet, but he did want them.

He damn well wanted it all.

The blue sky overhead gave way to sunshine peeking through bright white streaks, and by the time the official dinner rolled around, tall thunderstorm clouds filled the sky from one side of the horizon to the other.

Jace tracked down Cassidy where she was holding court with Steph, Sophie, and some of the elders of the pack.

The ladies offered him knowing grins as he inched his way as close as possible to Cassidy's side.

"Good to see you back." Mary Daccoda offered an approving smile. "How are your parents enjoying themselves out in the Maritimes?"

Another part about having grown up in the community. Everyone knew everyone else, even if his parents had moved about the time Jace had headed to college. "Dad considered becoming a lobster fisherman, but Mom prefers he keep his paws firmly on shore. They're giving tours at the *Anne of Green Gables* house instead."

Mary laughed. She tilted her head toward Cassidy then winked. "Maybe they'll have a reason to come visit sometime soon."

He kept his expression mellow. "Good to see you all again. Excuse us."

Jace wrapped his fingers around Cassidy's and tugged lightly.

She leaned into him but kept her attention on the woman in front of her until she'd finished speaking.

"Sounds like a lot of fun," Cassidy said to the woman. Parker? Paller? Some name like that. "We'll be sure to let Stacy know as well. Steph's sister and her boys will be here in less than a week. I know they're very excited to meet others their age."

"I'll make sure you get the information about when and where," Sophie promised.

Jace found himself the center of female attention. A half dozen sets of inquiring gazes looked him up and down. A few women noticed his and Cassidy's fingers tangled together and smiled.

Stephanie waved them off. "Go do whatever. Sophie and I are going to make big plans for a—"

A flash of lightning danced across the sky, followed seconds later by an enormous boom of thunder.

"They said the storm would be here before nightfall." Mary looked up expectantly as more flashes arrived along with a thickening wind. "That's my cue to head home before the rain hits. Thanks for the fun, Cassidy. Stephanie. Timberwolf Lodge is going to do fine under your management."

"Thanks for the vote of confidence," Stephanie said. She glanced up as another boom rang out. "Whoa. That came on fast."

Everyone who'd gathered scattered quickly. Camp chairs were folded, picnic baskets closed, children scooped up or herded toward vehicles. Others of the pack stripped down, tucking their clothes into the totes at the edge of the gathering that Blue had placed there in the morning. They shifted and then, as singles, couples, or families, headed into the trees and raced for home.

"That's so amazing." Cassidy leaned into him. Her eyes widened as she watched with a keen interest. "Will they be safe?"

"They're wolves," he reminded her. "They'll be fine. It's pretty exhilarating to be out in a storm—although my wolf isn't a fan of wet fur."

A moment later the beach and grassy areas were nearly empty, which was a good thing because the skies opened and the rain fell as if dropped from a bucket.

Instantly soaked, Cassidy tugged Jace with her toward the house. "Come on."

He pulled back slightly. "Afraid of a little water?"

"Heck no." She twirled, her soaking wet hair flying out in an arc as she spun. "I love the rain. You're the one who said you'd melt if you got wet."

"Oh, a challenge, is it?"

She grinned at him, rivulets of water pouring down her face.

He lifted her fingers to his lips and kissed her knuckles softly before tipping his head toward the forest. "Come on, then. I've got something to show you."

WANDERING into the woods while a storm raged down on them had to be one of the most impulsive actions Cassidy had ever done.

But the thrill of excitement inside her matched the growing pulse of need, and she raced beside Jace with the eagerness of a teenager on the last day of school.

It had been a good day. No, it had been a great day. She had noticed some of the pack members she'd met on Sunday hadn't showed up. They must be the ones who supported Del as Alpha.

But everybody who had come up to Timberwolf Lodge that day had been positive and welcoming—after she'd dealt with Emma and her catty friend. How anybody could be mean to Sophie, Cassidy could not comprehend.

But that world faded away as Jace led her to the right, skimming the edge of the trees instead of delving deeper.

"You're taking me in a big circle," she accused.

"There's a reason, and you'll like it," he promised.

Everything she owned was soaked. Overhead, the sky continued to put on a dazzling light show with rumbling sound effects. One particularly bright flash lit up the world as Jace pulled her to a stop beside a ladder.

Above their heads was a multilevel tree house. "Get out."

He gestured to the ladder. "We used to have one here years ago. Blue and I spent the last couple of nights fixing it up. We wanted it in place before Stacy's kids got here. Kids need a place of their own."

Cassidy made sure she had a firm grip on the slick rungs as she made her way skyward. When her head poked through the trapdoor into the main section of the tree house, she whistled in admiration. "Damn. Now I want a tree house."

Jace crowded after her, grinning as he lowered the trapdoor behind them and blocked out the wind. "Maybe if you're a good auntie, they'll let you borrow it sometimes."

Another flash of lightning went off in the distance, the bright white light filling the window and lighting the interior. It was plain and simple, but there were a few shelves and a bunch of cushions. Cassidy could already imagine how much fun the boys would have playing in the space.

They sat on the floor. Jace curled himself around her and pressed a kiss to the side of her neck. "You were amazing today."

All the shivers and sexy thoughts she'd had every time she'd spotted him that day came flooding back in. Cassidy separated his wet T-shirt from his body and peeled it over his head. The warmth of his torso against her fingertips was like a furnace. "I want you."

He stole away her top and then pressed his palms to her

cheeks, kissing her gently. Her lips, her jaw. The sweet spot under her ear. "You've got me."

Peeling out of their wet clothes took extra long because they kept getting wrapped up in each other. Hands that were supposedly helping to disrobe paused to caress. To tease.

Outside, the storm raged, thunder rattling overhead. But inside, heat grew. Jace reverently caressed her breasts, pulling her close until he could taste and nibble on her nipples. He sat up and pulled her into his lap, and she curled her arms around his shoulders, arching against him.

Cassidy closed her eyes, and a wildness stirred inside her. The sensation of being in Jace's arms was somehow meshed with images of wolves running. As he caressed her skin, she felt the wind sliding through her fur.

As he lay back and rolled her on top of him, she knew she was there in the treehouse with him. Hot and heavy and aching with need and lust. She rocked her hips, the thick length of his cock gliding under her sex. A temptation she was eager to enjoy.

Yet there was also the feel of rocks and earth under her paws. The bright tang of ozone from the storm in her nostrils. The low howl of a wolf calling to his mate.

She looked down and saw the deep blue of his eyes shimmering with silver. Saw his wolf. "You're beautiful," she whispered.

He pressed his fingers into the skin at her hips, rocking her over him. "I'm yours."

She took him inside her, surrounding him in one smooth motion.

It was like being filled with the storm. Pleasure skyrocketed, and she reveled in the hedonistic sensations teasing her inside and out. Cassidy marvelled at the mental images of two wolves, pale white and speckled grey. Wolves loving, tangled around each other.

Him—and her. Impossible, magical.

Perfect.

Jace curled himself upward and wrapped his arms around her. With their bodies still intimately connected, his lips took hers with a hunger that was beyond human. Cassidy kissed him back. Holding on tight, she accepted the taking and gave as good as she got, and together they spiraled upward toward the moment of breaking.

He's mine.

The thought came even as pleasure ripped his name from her lips.

Jace buried his face in her neck and growled as his release took control. Pulsing, rippling. A full-body experience that tangled them together and left them panting in each other's arms.

When Cassidy finally blinked her eyes open, it was to discover Jace grinning up at her. He brushed her hair back behind her ear. "Well, hello there."

He lay on his back on the hardwood floor of the tree house. She was using him as a mattress, her hands pressed to his chest. Under her palms, his still rapidly pulsing heart beat out a wild tempo.

So much to take in. So much to still understand. "That was pretty amazing sex."

"Agreed." He pulled her closer until he could nuzzle against her neck. "God, I love the smell of you right here. Just makes me wild."

"Give me five minutes," she warned.

Jace chuckled. "That's supposed to be my line."

"Hey, I'm not used to having visions while I'm having sex."

His smile only got bigger. "Nice to know I bring something new to the game."

She stared at him, the joy and pleasure inside her stealing toward seriousness. "This isn't ordinary, everyday awesome sex, is it?"

He shifted his head slightly. "No. But I don't want it to be. Do you?"

The connection between them kept growing. Cassidy couldn't deny it.

Didn't want to.

It seemed odd to come right out and ask, but it was the only way to be sure. "Are we mates? Fated or otherwise?"

Jace didn't hesitate. He curled himself upright until she sat in his lap, his arms around her. "Yes. But that doesn't mean this is all decided without you. I'm in—one hundred percent. The rest of it is up to you. When you're ready."

It's too quick. That was Cassidy's first thought, and it was true.

But she pressed her palm to his cheek and stared into those beautiful eyes, knowing *no* wasn't the whole answer. "I'm nearly there," she told him.

He could've been hurt by her statement. He could've tried to argue or convince her, but instead, he smiled.

"I'm glad. When you're ready," he repeated. "I'll be there to catch you. Forever and always."

Jace squeezed her tight, and Cassidy held on to him. The beat of their hearts fell into a matching rhythm as they sat high in the trees with the rain pouring all around them.

She held on and hoped.

16

"Tell me this isn't typical weather." Stephanie flounced into the living room, then swooned onto the couch next to Blue. "I'm not a duck. This would be lovely weather for a duck, but I prefer my humidity at something less than maximum saturation."

"It's not typical," Blue assured her. He held out the magazine they were consulting for furniture ideas. "Which do you like better, with or without armrests?"

Stephanie sighed dramatically again, then slid over to consider the options. "At least we have things to do while we're waiting for the rain to stop."

"Other than the things outside that aren't getting done." Cassidy turned and stared out the window again, admitting to herself she was pouting. "We were progressing so well."

"We have time," Steph assured her. She sat up and patted the open space beside her. "Come here. Blue and I were talking this morning, and I think he had a good idea."

The two of them were always talking, which Cassidy found rather cute.

Blue was so earnest and yet happy-go-lucky. It was nice to have him around. Especially in the past few days when he'd been a notable contrast to Jace. Who was not there at the moment, having slunk off to do some broody alpha stuff, she assumed.

The moment they had shared in the trees had been magical—literally. And now, days later, things were still very good between them, but Jace seemed distracted. Even more so than her.

She shook her head and gave Steph her attention. "Sorry."

"It's okay." Stephanie patted her leg. "Here's what we're thinking. Stacy arrives in the next couple of days. Depending on how the weather is, she'll want to let the kids have some time to settle in so they feel like this is home. Blue thinks the stuff we ordered for renovations inside the house should be here the Friday after Canada Day."

"Still a week away," Cassidy grumbled.

"Which is plenty of time for us to prep the rooms that are getting renovated," Blue pointed out. "If we give ourselves all of July to get the house ready as much as needed, along with a couple of the cottages, we could offer bookings for the last week of August and the September long weekend. Just to some of the old-timers who have expressed interest in coming out."

"We have a year to prove ourselves," Stephanie reminded her. "I think Blue's idea is a good one. We get the first families out, grab their feedback on what needs to improve, and then we spend the rest of the fall and winter making everything sparkle."

"Winter guests are a thing. Especially for wolves. So the next set of guests could start in December or over the holidays." Blue held up his hands. "Is it a plan?"

Cassidy considered. Their current expenses were low, other than the materials they purchased. It wasn't as if they had to scramble to pay rent. And with the work Jace had done once again hooking up the solar panel system that had been disconnected, the utility bill wasn't going to be too bad either. "I can see the wisdom in doing a soft opening. I'd like to get at least one group out for Thanksgiving, though, if that's possible. And then limited winter guests as we figure out the routine."

"I like it." Stephanie nodded. "And it'll also work well for Stacy because she'll have time to get the boys settled into the school year without the pressure of cooking for a full house."

"And your spa?" Cassidy asked.

Her friend lit up the room with her smile. "I won't have everything in place at the start, but I'll go slow and steady. If we have guests, I can arrange something to make their stay special."

In spite of the rain coming down outside, Cassidy's spirits lifted. "Okay. We need to figure out if Jace will be able—"

She stalled out. What was she supposed to say right now? If Jace was able to stay? If the pack got back in balance?

If he wasn't dead by then?

Blue rose to his feet, and suddenly Cassidy was enveloped in a huge hug. Very brotherly, very comforting.

"He's going to be okay," Blue assured her.

"I believe that. But I also kind of want to know Del's going to be okay as well, because the whole wolfy *rip each other limb from limb* idea isn't sitting great."

And the longer it took until things got resolved, the worse she felt.

The massive front door flew open and bounced off the wall. She turned to curse and discovered Jace stalking in. His eyes glowed bright red.

Blue threw his hands in the air and backed away from Cassidy as if she were a hot potato.

Oh, hell no.

Cassidy met Jace in the middle of the room, fisting her hand in the front of his shirt. "If even a single one of your brain cells is leaning toward hurting Blue for hugging me, you and I are going to have words."

Jace picked her up, threw her over his shoulder, and raced up the stairs.

"Dammit, Jace. Put me down. What the hell is wrong with you?"

He shoved through her bedroom door, dropped her on the mattress, and crowded over her. Then he buried his face in her neck and breathed in deep.

It really pissed her off how much she liked that. "I'm mad at you right now," she informed him. "Stop doing that thing that makes my toes curl when I'm mad at you."

He whispered something so softly she didn't hear what he said.

Cassidy threaded her fingers through his hair and tugged, pulling his head back far enough that their gazes met. "What?"

"I issued the challenge. Del and I meet tomorrow night to decide the leadership of the pack."

Oh, damn.

"Okay." Cassidy nodded, loosening her grip and stroking him. Running her fingers through his hair and petting him as he basically rubbed himself all over her like a giant house cat. "Okay."

Because it had to be. On every level, it had to be okay

because Cassidy couldn't imagine a world without Jace. This world, the one she'd fallen in love with in an amazingly short amount of time.

He held her, and he stroked her, and one thing led to another until they were twined together intimately. Giving to each other and taking as they needed.

It didn't change what was going to happen, but it made the here and now what it was supposed to be.

They were at the breakfast table the next morning when Stephanie asked the all-important question. "Where does this go down?"

"I issued the challenge, so Del picks the spot. He chose Wilson's meadow." His hand squeezed Cassidy's thigh. "It's going to be okay. I've got a plan."

Good thing one of them did. Her heart was in her throat, and she didn't know how she would make it through the rest of the day waiting for the challenge to happen. "I'm going to be there. Just in case there's some rule about humans not being allowed, I'm letting you know I'm going to be there."

He smiled. The first real true smile she'd seen on his face in days. "Babe, no one would dare think of keeping you away."

JACE COULDN'T REMEMBER another time when it had rained for so many days in a row in June. Which made the prospect of the challenge not only more difficult but infuriated his wolf on a whole different level.

He had to fight? No problem. Get wet? That pissed him off.

He stood at the side of the clearing, the pack members

who came to witness slowly filling spaces along the tree line. Before him was the large opening with shorter grass where they'd meet.

Blue left Cassidy and Stephanie standing with Sophie and came over to join Jace. "Not that you need it, but good luck."

Jace glanced at Cassidy, proud to see how she stood straight and tall amid those gathered as if she belonged. As if she knew. "Shouldn't you be staying neutral and not talking to me right now?"

Blue made a rude noise. "Please. Everybody knows I think you should be leading. If me talking to you is enough to make this barbaric ritual shorter, so be it."

On the other side of the clearing, Del was taking off his shirt.

"I was kind of hoping to rip one of his suits apart," Jace admitted, working to remove his clothes as well.

"You could ask for one as a bonus when you spare his life," Blue suggested. He patted his hand firmly on Jace's shoulder, gaze intent. "Keep control of your wolf. Del's done a decent job, all things considered. I think you'd regret it if you tore out his jugular."

"He's staring at Stephanie again," Jace said dryly.

"On the other hand, kick him in the balls a few times for me." Blue saluted then marched back to where the women waited.

A moment's pause as those who'd gathered quieted.

The rain continued to fall, soaking the ground so heavily that when Jace finished stripping and walked forward to meet Del in the middle of the clearing, mud squished up between his toes with every step.

Even Del's neatly trimmed hair was soaked enough to look unruly.

Del lifted his chin. "You've issued a challenge to my leadership. I accept, but I also offer leniency if you want to back out now."

"Blow me," Jace offered.

Del grinned. "Cocky bastard. I'll try to stop after you're incapacitated, but there's no guarantee." His gaze narrowed and turned dark. "And the great part is, with you out of the picture, Cassidy might—"

Jace saw red before the sentence was even over. His hand shot out, and his fingers wrapped around Del's throat.

The next second, Jace held a handful of fur, and razor-sharp teeth came dangerously close to his wrist.

Jace shifted, putting them back on an even playing field. Scrambling with teeth and claws to get a purchase in the mud as they lunged forward and swayed back. Jace ignored everything outside the circle.

He knew Cassidy was there—could feel she was there with everything in him. He knew Blue was there, giving the quiet support that had always been a part of their relationship. The laughing joy that was the newcomer Stephanie. And all the pack members Jace had been getting to know all over again during the past weeks.

They were there. He felt them, felt their support.

But the growling powerhouse in front of him was his highest priority.

Del feinted to the right then lurched left. Jace anticipated the move but reacted too slowly when the motion turned into a flip and then a swipe of claws. Pain raked his shoulder, streaking all the way down to his paw.

Before him, his cousin bared his teeth in a wolfish smile of satisfaction for drawing first blood.

Jace flew at him, twisting in midair, swinging his teeth in the hopes of connecting with a body part he could hang on to. He got a small slice of Del's haunch, and his low yip of pain made Jace's wolf want to beat his chest with pride.

Another rattle of thunder overhead, and the rain doubled in intensity, falling so hard that the crowds on the edge of the field vanished behind a curtain of water. Jace's senses filled with white noise—nothing but water. No scents but the crushed grass underfoot and the watered-down iron of blood.

Del crashed into him from the left. Jace snapped his teeth on empty air. He twisted, lunged, and smashed his head into something solid that grunted before it rolled away.

He took a chance, rolling and swinging in the hopes of catching Del unaware before his cousin found his feet. The instant Jace closed his jaws around fur, he realized the trap. Del had him by the leg as well. Both in a position to hurt each other without gaining an advantage.

A long low howl split the air. Feeble, weak.

Both Jace and Del froze, teeth digging into each other's fur, but held on without ripping.

Another cry, the faintest call of a frightened young wolf.

Jace let go. Del pulled away at the same instant. And then they were off, out of the challenge circle and breaking through the trees side by side.

Somewhere ahead of them, something had gone completely wrong. The rain eased off barely enough that they could see the trail, sprinting down it, jumping the obstacles flying at them from either side. Behind him, Jace heard another wolf racing after them and sensed it was Blue.

Moments later, they found it. A minivan stuck in the middle of the broken-down bridge. The culvert underneath had washed away, one side support had vanished, and the back wheels of the van were being forced down the shallow river by the excess current.

Jace glanced in the window and spotted a shockingly familiar face. It couldn't be Stephanie, which meant this was her sister, Stacy. He shifted on the spot, rushing forward to grab for the van door.

Another flood of water cascaded down the river and tore the wheels from their moorings, making the van slide farther into the river.

"Stacy. Where are the kids?" Jace shouted.

She unrolled the window just as the engine cut out. She pointed behind her. "Help me."

Beside him, Del took a running start, then flew to land on the roof of the van. He shifted out of his wolf and, clinging to the rocking van, leaned over. "Can you open the doors?"

Stacy shook her head. "I can get them out the window. Stay there."

She vanished into the back, crawling over the driver's seat. A moment later, a young boy with a mess of bright red hair stuck his head out the window, big blue eyes wide with fear.

"You're okay. Del is going to grab you then send you to me. Be brave," Jace shouted.

Del nodded. He lay down on the roof and reached in to grab the little boy's hands.

A second later, he had the kid hauled up on the roof. "Curl up in a ball," Del ordered. "Like doing a cannonball at the swimming pool."

The van rocked. Del stumbled for a second, recovered his balance then sent the child flying into Jace's arms.

Blue was there. He took the boy from Jace, even as Del pulled a younger child from the window.

A second time Del threw. Jace caught the kid in a strange wilderness baseball game with more at stake than simple scores.

Stacy was back at the window, tears pouring down her face. "I can't get Colt to come. He's in his wolf form, and he's really scared."

The van rocked, sliding farther into the river. The back wheels must've hit a deeper spot because the van began to roll onto its side. Stacy backed away from the window with fear.

Del reached in and caught her wrist. "We'll get him. But you're coming out now."

She struggled. "*No.* Not without my son."

The van moved rapidly as the water level rose and forced the vehicle farther into the current. Trees from upstream that had been pushed over smashed into the metal frame. In spite of her protests, Del hauled Stacy to the roof as the entire vehicle began to roll.

Del picked up Stacy and jumped, vanishing from Jace's sight on the other side of the river.

Another long sorrowful howl echoed. Heartbreaking and young.

Jace didn't think, just moved. He tore forward, shifting as he moved. His wolf dove through the open window right before the van tilted and the side hit the water.

It was dark in the van, which bounced as it banged off rocks and trees. Water filled the interior to the halfway point as the van continued to be tossed downstream. Jace shifted back again, exhaustion beginning to set in as he crawled over seat backs. He passed floating Hot Wheels cars and discarded gummy-bear wrappers.

Huddled on top of the farthest backrest Colt shivered in his wolf form.

Another hard bounce, and Colt slipped. Jace caught him against his body and worked his way back to the passenger door. "I got you. This isn't much fun, so let's get you back to your mom."

The water kept rising as the van scraped over rocks and was pounded by passing logs. Jace braced his back and used his feet to shove the sliding passenger door open far enough to crawl on top.

Uneven light broke overhead, the cloud cover and monsoon-like rain darkening the sky. Jace peered at the riverbank, relieved to discover Blue tracking the van's progress. "Batter up," he called.

"Damn right," Blue called back. "Hey, Colt. Don't worry. I've got a big catcher's mitt."

The wolf in Jace's arms shivered but focused intently on Blue.

"Stay in your wolf form until you land, kid. It'll make things easier," Jace warned. He pulled back his arm to prepare the throw.

A tree smashed into the front of the van, riding up and over, aimed straight at Jace's feet. A crash was inevitable, but before he fell, Jace hurled Colt toward Blue on the shore.

Jace snatched at the rapidly moving timber in hopes that it would get trapped against the van and be stuck in one place.

No such luck. As the limb under his fingers shifted, Jace scrambled to find his balance. He teetered on one foot, nearly recovered, when, in his peripheral vision, something massive moved.

Damn it. He was fucking toast.

The log came straight for Jace, took his feet out from under him, and sent him crashing into the dirty, swirling water. The sound of Cassidy's cry echoed in his ears before his head went under.

Something crashed into his temple, and everything went dark.

17

Minutes earlier...

The fight had been terrifying, especially when blood appeared, painting both Jace and Del with red so that Cassidy didn't know which one of them was hurt. And while her heart pounded for Jace, she didn't want Del dead either. She didn't want Jace to have to live with the knowledge that he'd killed his cousin.

Adrenaline pumped through her as hard and fast as if she were fighting herself, and the moment the two bit down on each other, she swore she felt it in her own limbs.

Then the howl rang out—

"Oh my God. That's Colt." Instantly, Stephanie caught Blue by the shoulders and shoved him forward, breaking the challenge circle. "That's my nephew howling. Where is he? Find him."

Blue moved so fast he was a blur. The two wolves in the middle of the challenge field moved even faster. Jace and

Del broke apart from each other and disappeared into the trees, Blue a faint shadow on their heels.

The remaining group swayed on their feet, shock rippling through them.

Cassidy shook her head, struggling to think. "What's down that way? Is there a trail? A road?"

Sophie popped up beside her. "A really old road. The old access to Timberwolf Lodge. But it hasn't been used in years. Not since the bridge was decommissioned."

"Well, somebody tried to use it today," Cassidy snarled before twirling toward the crowd and calling out orders. "If you can help, follow Jace and Del. Otherwise, find some shelter or go to Timberwolf Lodge. We'll let you know as soon as we have news."

Shockingly, everyone listened, dispersing in different directions.

Sophie caught hold of Cassidy's arm. "You can't run as fast as I can when I'm a wolf, so I'll stay human. Come on. I know a shortcut down to the old bridge."

Miserably wet, fear drenching her limbs, Cassidy followed the petite woman. Stephanie followed behind, the two of them breathing heavily without speaking, saving their energy to try and keep up.

The rain lightened just enough that they could make their way through the rain-slicked branches before popping out on an old road above a washed-out bridge.

"*Auntie Steph.*"

Blue raced up with Stacy's youngest boys clinging to him. "Hand off. I'll be back."

Steph snatched up Blaze, Cassidy grabbed Ace, and Blue was gone, racing up the riverbank again.

On the other side of the river, the small forms of Del and Stacy were barely visible as the rain continued to fall.

Cassidy could have sworn she saw Stacy deck Del before she raced back toward the river. He chased after her, scooped her up over his shoulder and carried her, still struggling, toward the bridge.

The van now lay on its side in the middle of the river. When Jace's head popped up through the barely open passenger door, a wolf cub in his arms, relief rushed through Cassidy.

Which meant seeing the trees bear down on the van in slow motion was something out of a horror movie. Colt flew through the air and landed in Blue's arms, knocking the man to his butt. Jace slid along the roof, a massive tree limb tipping him sideways.

Jace vanished over the edge of the van.

She screamed, but even as the sound hung on the air, Cassidy was already moving. "Jace."

Another sharp phantom pain struck, as if she were being pierced in the temple by a sharp blade. She wavered on her feet for a second then forced herself upright.

Stephanie grabbed her arm. "Careful, Cass."

Cassidy passed Ace over. "I'm going after him."

She sprinted past Blue, astonishment on his face as he turned toward her, his arms full of preteen wolf. "*Cassidy.*"

"Stay with the boys," she ordered, running down the trail beside the river, glancing at the roaring water in the hopes that she'd see Jace's head pop up.

She rounded the bend, and the river widened. No longer twenty feet across but a huge expanse full of tumbling debris.

Hopelessness wrapped around her, and she closed her eyes. "Jace."

She saw him. And her wolf.

There, with her eyes closed, she saw the white wolf

she'd followed in her dreams bump noses with Jace. He lay motionless at the edge of the river. Not her section of river but somewhere else, and Cassidy opened her eyes, desperate to find him.

The magic remained. It would've done no good to stay still and track him with the wolf in her mind only. Now, even with her eyes open, the vision of her wolf glided noiselessly on the trail ahead of her. Weaving to the side before disappearing into the brush.

No doubt. No fear. Cassidy followed, sprinting into the darkness.

Within seconds, she was seeing double. The trees and the trail in front of her were clear enough that she could stay on her human feet and avoid stumbling. And at the same time, she was the wolf, sniffing, looking. Listening for any trace of Jace.

She rounded the corner and burst from the rain-soaked trees.

At the side of the river, a dark patch of fur lay with limbs tangled in a small rosebush that had been torn up by the roots. Cassidy hurried forward and shoved away the debris.

"Jace." She leaned in close and pressed a hand to his chest, praying for some sign of life.

Had he moved? She leaned in closer.

His tongue came out and managed to hit her from her chin to the top of her forehead.

Cassidy laughed, relief flooding in as she pressed a kiss to his bruised temple. "You'd better have magical, super healing powers, buster, or I'm going to be very pissed at you."

And then, the most wonderful thing happened. Jace opened his eyes, and she fell in love. Completely. Totally.

It might be fate, but it was real.

JACE ACHED EVERYWHERE. There was water in his ears, his tail was likely broken, and as he shifted back to human form, a splinter the size of a baseball bat dug into his right ass cheek, but those were the smallest of his worries.

He was alive, and Cassidy was there, kissing him and holding him as if she planned to stay a while.

Which was wonderful and meant he could deal with some other things first.

"Is Colt okay?" Damn, his voice sounded like shit.

Cassidy pressed a hand to his cheek. "Don't talk. Last I saw he was fine."

"He's more than fine," Blue said.

Jace twisted his head and worked to focus on his cousin, who had appeared out of the trees to join them.

Blue shook his head but reached down and held out a hand. "All the kids and Stacy are safe. You're the biggest mess. Let's get you back to the gathering. You've got some shit to finish."

"He's not fighting anymore." Cassidy's anger burned so white-hot, Jace felt it down to his toes.

He rocked for a moment, then straightened his spine and stood firmly, despite the aches. It wasn't good to show weakness in front of his mate when she was this riled up.

He agreed, though. "No. I'm not fighting. But Blue is right. There's something that needs to be finished."

No way was he walking through the trees on bare human feet. He shifted, nudged Cassidy ahead of him, then followed behind her as Blue led them back to the challenge grounds.

Stacy was there, her three boys clutched at her side. Colt was still in his wolf form, and Jace went forward to touch his nose to the kid's.

Colt shifted to human form, his eyes wide. He stayed low, one hand rising tentatively to stroke Jace's shoulder. "I was scared," he whispered. "But I did what you said."

Silently, Jace bumped him with his head, offering approval. There'd be time for words later, but for now, Colt smiled and let out a shaky sigh.

Seconds later, Jace returned to the center of the clearing where Del waited, already in human form.

Jace shifted back. He met his cousin's gaze squarely. "There's another way to do this," he offered. "It doesn't have to be all or nothing."

Incredibly, Del's attention was not on Jace but glued to Stacy and the boys at the side of the clearing. "You saved him. I couldn't, but you saved him."

"*We* saved them. We did what needed to be done, and that's what a leadership team does." Jace widened his stance and folded his arms over his chest. "You did something very difficult to start your time as Alpha, and you've led as best you could. But you were made for something different, Del."

That was enough to get his cousin's attention. He raised a brow.

Jace shrugged softly. "Your profession gives it away. You're a fighter. You fight for justice, and you do a good job of it. Which makes me think you'd do a really good job of being Enforcer for the pack."

Del's eyes widened. "Enforcer?"

"Well, Blue's got the Omega position all sewn up since neither you nor I can pull off the magical gobbledygook he does. And my wolf is pretty determined to be Alpha. But you need to be part of the team."

His cousin's gaze drifted once again to where the women waited, listening intently.

Del twisted back. "I agree that Blue is our Omega. And I like the idea of Enforcer. But I think you need to admit you're not the only Alpha around these parts."

Jace's mate frowned, obviously misinterpreting. Just the look of determination on Cassidy's face made it easy to do the next thing.

Jace looked Del straight in the eyes. "You're right. Cassidy? Would you come here, babe?"

Surprise flashed across her face.

At her side, Stephanie listened intently as Blue leaned in close and whispered in her ear. Her lips turned up in a curl, and she put her arms around Cassidy's shoulders, then pushed her toward the middle. "Go on. You know you want to talk some sense into the two of them."

Cassidy might've been shocked to be put on the spot, but it was no more than two steps toward them when her shoulders went back and her chin lifted. She walked all the way up and deliberately turned so she stood by his side and a half inch in front of him. As if daring Del to make a move.

Del grinned. His gaze flashed to Jace's then back to Cassidy. "Forgive me if I get formal. It's always good to dot the i's and cross the t's."

Cassidy waited warily.

Del twisted slowly, getting the attention of the wolves who had returned or had never left. And then, with all eyes on him, he pressed a hand to his chest and spoke in a clear voice. "I have given of myself as Alpha for this pack, but I now pass on that responsibility and privilege. I take up the mantle of Enforcer and will use my energies and, if need be, my life to protect the pack. There will be no further challenge from this quarter as I accept the rule of my Alphas." As Del dipped his chin toward her, Jace heard Cassidy's heart rate pick up.

He reached over and tangled his fingers with hers, still smiling because this was right.

Del glanced at her, still bowing. He spoke quietly this time. "Right now, it would be good if you said something along the lines of 'we accept your service and—'"

"Endless groveling?" Jace suggested.

Del frowned. "You're such a jackass."

"That's *Alpha* jackass to you," Jace corrected him. "But I suggest you don't call my mate a jackass if you'd like to keep your head on your shoulders. You can call her *Alpha overlord*, or *Alpha supreme*, or *Alpha extraordinaire*."

Cassidy's grip on Jace's fingers tightened like a vise. "You're going to be the *Enforcer* for the pack," she said to Del, half a question, half a statement.

"As long as you and Jace are the Alphas, yes," Del said firmly.

Her mouth hung open for a moment. "Oh. Wow."

For the first time in ages, Del looked Jace full in the eyes, and they exchanged a grin. Peacefulness rushed into Jace, a sense of rightness settling between them. And when Blue sauntered forward with that indolent way of his, the final missing piece clicked into place.

They were finally a pack the way they were supposed to be. There was still a lot to figure out, but this team at the root of it, this was right.

Now he had to convince Cassidy to become his mate. Not just his co-leader but his in every way.

Because only then could he be completely hers.

18

____

*B*ack at Timberwolf Lodge, Stephanie and Blue took Stacy and the boys on a tour that included hot baths and a lot of hugs. Del commandeered a group of wolves to head with him to the river. He promised to rescue as much of their stuff out of the van as possible.

Cassidy took charge of Jace. Because he obviously needed a keeper.

"I can't believe you stood there and did all that unthinking *we're all fine, I'm a macho wolf* bullshit while you were bleeding." She shoved him back into the shower. "Stay there. You've still got dirt in the claw marks on your hip, and let me say that is not a phrase I ever expected to nonchalantly utter."

Jace turned obediently and let her soap him up with antibacterial bubbles. "My wolf laughs in the face of germs."

"Unless you can tell me how wolf physiology allows you to not suffer from septic bacteria, you will stay still until I tell you otherwise."

Wisely, he stayed silent. But every time she glanced at

him, he was grinning so hard he might as well have been laughing.

Finally, she stood before jerking him out of the shower and shoving a towel into his arms. "Dry yourself off."

Jace mock pouted. "I thought you'd help me."

She ignored him, stripped off the rest of her things, and went into the shower to clean herself up.

She was under the hot stream, letting the water roll down her face, when he stepped in behind her.

Strong arms wrapped around her, his cheek coming to rest against hers. "I can tell you're crying, even with the water hitting your face like that."

She turned so she could rest her forehead against his chest. "You scared me," she admitted. "You scared me a lot."

He tucked his fingers under her chin and lifted her face to his. "And here I thought you were upset because I went and made you Alpha without asking you first."

He kissed her softly before separating just far enough to gaze intently into her eyes.

There was worry there, so she hurried to reassure him. "The Alpha thing is very strange, but it also feels right. I think you were brilliant in how you handled that. I wish you would've thought of it before you and Del started carving each other up."

He brushed at her cheek. "So these are really just about my furry side taking a dunk in the river?"

"Shifter, not furry." He laughed, like she'd intended. Then she took her time and thought it through. "We're connected. I can't deny that, and I don't want to. The whole idea of fated mates sounds impossible, yet so does people who turn into wolves." She wrapped her arms around his neck and pulled him in close. Hugging him, holding him. When she let go, she tilted her head toward the bedroom.

"Let's dry off. I'll tell you the rest once my toes are no longer turning into prunes."

Five minutes later they were dressed in comfortable cotton. Jace leaned against the headboard, while Cassidy sat cross-legged in the middle of the bed.

He held out a hand, and she took it before resting their linked fingers on her knee. "I used my wolf to find you."

This time his eyes widened. "What?"

She dipped her chin. "You took me running that one night. I stood in one place, and my wolf ranged all over the valley. But the second time, we were making love, and our wolves were—" She looked into his eyes, and yes, it was there again. That mischievous expression that said he remembered every minute as clearly as she did. "Our wolves were getting frisky. So I guess I was kind of moving in both places."

"Definitely moving," he agreed.

She wiggled up onto her knees. "When you vanished into the water, I couldn't simply stand there and let my wolf explore alone. And it wasn't fun and playful like the second time. But I needed her, and she was there—my wolf. Somehow we were together, and she led me all the way to where you were."

He nodded. Waited.

"I knew. *We* knew how to find you."

He moved to cup her cheek. "That's amazing. And I'm not surprised. Not one bit. I knew you were special and exactly right for me."

Cassidy's heart fluttered. "Since the first moment I met you, I've felt as if we belong together. I know about animal attraction and passion for someone, but with you, it's different. Deeper."

He brushed his thumb over her lower lip. "Fated mates."

Which seemed like a phrase that should piss her off, but it absolutely did not. "It's not just fate," she insisted. "Not if I *choose* you."

~

SOME MOMENTS WERE ETCHED in his memory forever, and he already knew this would be one of them. Cassidy, her big green eyes so focused and intent on him as she brought him close and kissed him.

An invitation and a claiming all in one.

Jace twisted on the mattress until Cassidy rested against him. The soft curves of her body nestled against his torso, her hands wrapping around his back as they kissed. Explored. Agreed to please each other with shaking breaths and lingering tastes and tender caresses.

The clothes they'd pulled on vanished. It was hot enough in the bed with only naked skin. Got hotter still as Jace stroked his palms up her body and cupped her full breasts. With her nipples pebbling against his palms, Jace hummed happily.

She laughed. "It's official. You're a breast man."

"I'm a *you* man," he corrected. "God, I want to eat you up in one greedy bite."

"We have time. More than one bite is allowed."

Which meant since they were convenient, he started on her breasts. Nibbling on the soft undercurve, licking over each tip. Cassidy arched, clutching his head to her as he enjoyed the taste of her skin, the taste of anticipation as he worked his way farther down. Kissing her belly, teasing his tongue along the crease where her leg met her torso.

Cassidy squirmed and then sighed, her thighs falling apart in invitation as Jace kissed the top of her mound. "*Jace.*"

"Let me love you," he whispered.

He covered her with his mouth, tracing the edges of her clit gently. Over and over. She squirmed so hard under him, he pressed a hand over her belly to lock her in position.

He cupped a hand around her thigh, then eased upward. One finger stroked her wet folds before slipping inside.

Cassidy moaned, then groaned, then gave a shaky purr as he teased another finger in with the first. He curled them against the front of her sex, and she gasped in pleasure.

Jace grinned. "I like the noises you make."

"Come up here, and we can make some noises together," she offered.

"Ladies first."

He leaned up on an elbow, though, so he could watch. Cassidy met his gaze, and eyes wide open, gave him the gift of every moment of pleasure she experienced. When her orgasm rolled over her and she sighed happily, Jace grinned.

Then he moved and slid in deep before her body had stopped tightening. Which meant he was wrapped in a velvet fist that made the base of his spine tingle.

Cassidy held him with her eyes too. Sparkling bright, smart and aware. "I want to be your mate."

"You are. You will be," he promised.

"Not on some far-off day," she warned. "Today. I choose you, Jace. Your wolf. Your pack."

"*Our* pack." He thrust again, making them both moan. "I'll need to bite you."

Her eyes widened.

"Only a little," he promised. "And I hear it feels good."

She wrapped her legs around his hips and pulled him in, speeding up the rhythm of their lovemaking. Clearly saying she was on board and involved in all this.

"Yes." Cassidy dug her fingernails into his shoulders and scratched, and Jace's vision blurred. "Yes, bite me. Make me yours."

Pleasure was a glowing thing, wrapped around them and filling the room. Jace pumped hard and deep, ecstasy sliding up his spine and making his breath hitch.

He snuck a hand between them, covered her clit, and rubbed even as he pumped his cock harder. Deeper. Cassidy gasped, then growled and wiggled as close as possible.

"Jace." Her back bowed upward. Her sex clenched around him, and he moved. Teeth to her neck, a sharp, quick bite.

Extreme pleasure exploded through him, her taste on his tongue, his body in hers. Their minds connected so he felt every bit of the wild pleasure she experienced.

Outside the bedroom, and with joy pulsing through their veins, Jace saw them. A white wolf stood beside his grey one on a high ridge. The wind in their fur, noses bumping. Connected.

Mates.

Jace couldn't hold back any longer. He spoke, his voice deep and rough. "I love you."

A shiver raced over Cassidy's skin, but she lifted her eyes to his, and they were full of joy and wonder. "I love you too," she said clearly before echoing her earlier statement. "I choose you. Forever."

19

———

The breakfast table the next morning was a little fuller and a lot noisier.

"Hey, Mr. Blue." Six-year-old Blaze tugged on Blue's sleeve, his excitement over pancakes temporarily forgotten.

"Yeah, kiddo?" Blue turned every bit of attention on him.

"What do you call a wolf with a fever?"

Blue winked across the table at Colt. "I don't know. What do you call a wolf with a fever?"

Blaze leaned his hands on the table and answered with excitement, "A hot dog."

His brothers laughed like little hyenas, while Blue smacked a hand to his forehead.

Cassidy left the kids with Blue and snuck over to stand beside Stacy, who was cutting up oranges for the table. "How're you doing?"

Her friend motioned at her children. "They're safe. I've never been better."

Cassidy felt some guilt for having abandoned the rest of them the previous evening, but then again, a girl only got mated once. The mark on her neck still tingled, but it looked more like a tattoo than a bite even now, less than twelve hours later.

"Did Del find most of your stuff?"

Stacy's shoulders tightened. "Yes."

Jace strolled past before pausing to sneak his arm around Cassidy. Not so much a claiming but more as if he simply didn't want to be apart from her. "I'm glad you guys are all okay."

Her friend put the knife down, her hands quivering slightly as she carefully wiped them dry. Then she lifted her gaze to Jace's. "I can never repay you for what you did."

Jace brushed his knuckles over her cheek, wiping away a tear that had made a sudden break for it. "There's no debt between friends. There's no debt between family. There's no debt between pack, and you're all three. You and the boys."

A second later, Stacy had her arms wrapped around their shoulders, clinging to Jace and Cassidy as she fought for control. "I'm so glad we have you."

Cassidy squeezed her tight. Jace patted her on the back even as he spoke softly. "Let's get to breakfast before Thing One, Two, and Three get curious as to why their mama is upset."

"I'm not upset," Stacy insisted, letting them go and wiping her eyes dry with the back of her hand. "I'm so grateful you were there when that damn bridge gave way. I thought we were all done for."

At the counter, Stephanie finished loading the final pancakes onto a massive plate. She laid it on the table then tugged Stacy into the seat next to her. "I don't understand why you were on that road, though. I sent you directions."

"Three sets of directions," Stacy complained. "I had to

keep plugging new coordinates into the GPS. The last ones you sent are what I followed."

Stephanie shook her head. "Sissy, you really think I attempted technology and maps more than once? I sent you one copy—the same one we followed to get here, and that route was nowhere near the disaster zone."

Three sets of curious eyes turned their way, worry rising as the boys listened in. Cassidy hurried to redirect the conversation. "Well, however it happened, it turned out okay."

"It did." Jace pressed a kiss to Cassidy's nape, then dropped into the seat next to Colt, who stared at him with an awe usually reserved for superheroes. Jace examined the boys, gaze narrowing. "Ready for your first big test of the Jasper pack?"

Three heads dipped, their eyes wide.

"It's called the piggy stack challenge."

Stephanie snorted. "Oh, I can already see where this is going."

A loud knock was followed immediately by the front door slamming open and bouncing off the wall.

"Don't start piggy stacking without me." Marvin strolled in, an enormous platter balanced on one hand. He winked at Cassidy. "Hey, darling. I'd tell you I invited myself to breakfast, but that one told me to come." He pointed at Blue.

Everyone twisted in their seats. Blue lifted his hands in the air. "I knew Jace would issue a challenge, and Marvin's the only one who might be able to give him a run for his money."

Cassidy laughed then pulled another chair up to the table. "Okay. Make yourself at home. Oh, I forgot—you already did."

Marvin grinned.

The platter he carried turned out to be filled with crispy bacon.

Jace was showing the boys how to build a piggy stack—alternating layers of pancakes and bacon and then dousing the entire thing with maple syrup—when another knock sounded.

"Grand Central Station around here." Stacy hopped to her feet. "I'll get it," she insisted as Cassidy made a move to join her. "You need to be a judge for what I think is going to involve my boys and soon-to-be tummy aches."

Still, Cassidy watched with curiosity as Stacy strode to the door and pulled it open.

Del stood there, hands shoved in his pockets, gaze flying over the gathering then back to Stacy. "Hi."

She slammed the door shut and calmly walked back to the table.

Cassidy and Jace exchanged puzzled glances before Cassidy bounced up to open the door and poke her head outside.

Del stood there, rubbing his forehead.

"She hit you? I didn't think the door moved that fast."

He blinked then offered a weak smile. "Um, no. Just... came over to see how everyone is doing after yesterday's adventures."

Jace slipped up behind Cassidy, draping an arm over her shoulders. "Hey. You want to come in for breakfast?"

Del glanced into the room then blinked again. This time his gaze went to the mark on Cassidy's neck. "Oh, wow. Congrats, you two."

"Thanks." Jace nodded firmly then caught Del by the arm and tugged him into the room. "You're staying for breakfast."

"Ummm, but I'm not sure..."

"Mr. Jace? Colt shifted into a wolf. That's not fair. He can eat way more piggy stacks if he's a wolf," Blaze complained while Colt let out a series of delighted yips.

Jace laughed, tilting his head toward the chaos in the kitchen. "Come on, Enforcer. You can help enforce the rules around here."

He pushed Del ahead of them toward the table. The man went willingly, eager even as he found a chair next to five-year-old Ace.

Cassidy held Jace back before they took their own seats, her curiosity rising far enough she whispered in his ear. "What's up with them?" She flicked a finger between Stacy and Del.

Stacy picked up her chair and moved it a few inches farther from Del. Then she turned her back on him and became intensely interested in helping Blaze build an enormous piggy stack.

"No idea. Blue might know, but for now, I think we're safe to let it roll." Jace kissed Cassidy quickly then raised his voice. "I'm ready to take on all challengers."

The rest of the meal was full of good food, laughter, and a sense of family Cassidy was thrilled to experience.

She took a slow evaluation of the group. Her two best friends—here in a new place, ready to face the next stage of their adventure. They had begun to set down roots, even though they still had a long way to go to make the lodge a viable resort.

They had to get the approval of the Wilson pack—she'd realized that meant wolves, and not the Jasper ones—before next spring. It was doable, whoever it was they needed to impress.

Especially if the newcomers at the table were a part of

the solution. Blue, with his quick smile and gentle heart. Del, who'd turned out to be rock solid and fearless when he needed to be.

Marvin, the nanny moose—who could have guessed?

And Jace.

Cassidy met his gaze, and the spot on her neck tingled. Inside, something wild stretched. Her wolf? It was all so exciting, and she still had so much to learn about that part of her.

But it was Jace who made her heart skip a beat—his steady blue gaze like a slice of the sky, brushing her with the sweet, glorious freedom of fresh air and wilderness. His heart right there for her to see.

His love. Amazing. Wild.

Perfect, and all hers.

The whole change of circumstance made her grin. She'd been looking for a new place, better options. Could never have dreamed the Alpha option would be hers.

She slipped up to the table, settled in Jace's lap, and stole the final piece of bacon off his fork.

He waggled his brows at her then kissed her, ignoring the sound of small boys groaning dramatically at the public display of affection.

Yup, Cassidy thought as she pulled back and grinned at her mate and the others gathered at the table. It wasn't an option she'd ever dreamed of—

It was better.

EPILOGUE

The kids were herded outside by Blue, Jace, and Marvin to run off steam after eating far too many piggy stacks. Stephanie and Cassidy had vanished for a moment, headed to the office to check the delivery dates for supplies.

Which left Delaney Vezina—ousted pack Alpha, new pack Enforcer—a little bemused as he stood at the kitchen sink, hands in the dirty dishwater, scrubbing the breakfast cookware.

It was humbling yet perfect. Because the other person still in the room was Stacy, working silently as she cleared the table and stacked plates in the dishwasher.

God, he'd been a fool. The past weeks, every time he'd scented Stephanie, Del had wondered why she seemed *almost* right. Now it was crystal clear—it hadn't been Stephanie he'd been waiting for.

It was Stacy. *She* was his fated mate.

Which was perfect—*not*—since she hated his guts.

Del scrubbed a little harder at the bacon grease under

his fingers. Damn it anyway. It seemed it was one step forward, two steps back for him around here lately.

God, just being in the same room with her made his entire body ache.

He'd felt a hit of interest in Cassidy because of her strength. An intriguing tug toward Stephanie because of the confusing scent...

Stacy left both those sensations in the dust.

"You're going to scrub the bottom off that pan." She stood beside him, her golden-brown irises flashing with sunshine as she hesitantly offered him a slight smile.

Clumsy like a starstruck teen, he dropped the pan into the sink. The splash of soapy water sprayed out and soaked him from midchest down.

Stacy gasped and backed up. She'd been hit as well. Water soaked the front of her shirt, and he tore his gaze away from her breasts before he made matters worse by staring.

God, he wanted to stare. Wanted to strip her down and lick her clean with his tongue—

"Sorry. So sorry." He grabbed the hand towel and reached out to brush her dry, reconsidered, then handed the towel to her instead. "I'm so sorry."

"You said that already."

"I'll say it again if you want me to." Blathering, he was blathering. When the hell did he lose his balls and turn into a sniveling submissive?

Oh, right. When she'd decked him in the woods the previous night. Followed by her slamming the door in his face a couple of hours ago.

Stacy took the towel and dabbed it against her shirt, but her expression was thoughtful and then full of remorse. She looked him straight in the eye. "I'm the one who owes you an apology."

Del didn't move. "What?"

She took a deep breath, her gaze shaky, but she maintained eye contact. "Last night. I was upset at leaving Colt, but you did the right thing. You took me to safety, and even if"—her voice broke, but when he would have moved to comfort her, she held up a hand—"even if the worst had happened, and Colt had been trapped, you were right to get me to safety when you did. Me getting stuck in the van, both of us dying, would have left Ace and Blaze without their mom."

A cold chill raced over him. The idea of her or any of the boys being gone was wrong. So very wrong.

Stacy raced on. "I'm used to doing things on my own. My first husband was gone a lot on tour, so he let me run things at home pretty much like I wanted. And my second husband—" She shook her head. "Let's just say that by the end, I had to deal with a lot on my own there as well."

Del wanted to pick her up and hold her close. Wanted to hear everything that was wrong so he could make it right.

He had it so bad.

Stacy straightened, and her expression turned serious. "Listen to me. I'm babbling. You don't need to know that I went from the best husband in the world to the worst husband ever, but maybe that explains why being told what to do made my hackles rise."

"It was a stressful situation. I wasn't offended," he assured her.

"I'm saying you were right to haul me away, despite my protests. Thank you for making the decision I couldn't."

His feet were nailed to the floor as he was struck

motionless by shock. "I'm so glad it ended well, but thanks for being understanding."

"And I shouldn't have slammed the door in your face." Stacy swallowed hard. "I... Well, I guess we'll be sharing more secrets over the coming days, since Cassidy explained you're part of the pack leadership. This is my fresh start with the kids. Another fresh start," she said, wrinkling her nose in the most adorable way.

He'd heard bits. Knew her oldest son was from that military husband who'd died in service. Her younger two—their father sounded like a lot more trouble. "I don't need to know your secrets."

"No? Well, I guess not yet. But you do deserve an apology. I am sorry, and I'm glad I'm here to make it. I hope we can be friends going forward."

"Absolutely." They had to start somewhere. No way was he stopping at friends, though.

Stacy nodded. "I need friends." She laughed a little uneasily, setting up and taking over the washing. "Lots and lots of friends."

"You've got a good start," Del promised. "Not only because Cassidy is a rock and you and your sister seem amazing together. But the pack will be there for you too."

"Good. Good." Stacy nodded, but she was clearly distracted.

He was as well if he were honest.

His mate was right there, and he couldn't say a word. Not only was she just learning about wolf dynamics, but she needed time to adjust after her move. To settle in with the boys and make the lodge into their home.

To help her friends meet the challenge Auntie Rachel had laid out in the lottery giveaway and make Timberwolf Lodge a success.

His wolf stretched inside, eager to hunt. Eager to officially meet his mate. The one thing that could not happen anytime soon.

He and Stacy worked in silence, side by side, finishing the cleanup from breakfast. The entire time, though, Del plotted and planned. Created possibilities and discarded them.

She wiped the counter one last time, offered a shaky smile, then slipped from the room.

Delaney Vezina stood and watched her go, a decision and vow rising diamond strong. Stacy wanted a friend? Hell, they'd be friends all right. Then he'd woo her, win her, and prove they were meant to be lovers. Then mates, and then a family.

He wasn't always a betting man, but this? He was willing to wager everything he had, take a gamble, and make it happen.

Del had his sights on Stacy. Whatever it took—

He was all in.

◞◟

New York Times Bestselling Author Vivian Arend
brings you a light-hearted paranormal trilogy
Timberwolf Lodge.

WIN A WILDERNESS LODGE!

Ready for the chance of a lifetime? Enter now to become
the new owners of the Timberwolf Lodge located near
Jasper, Alberta. You'll have one year to meet the set
conditions and the lodge will be all yours!

Small print: (very, very, very small print)
Warning: Lodge may contain werewolves, fated mates, and
tons of shifter pack drama.
Good luck, and have fun! Don't die!

◞◟

Timberwolf Lodge
The Alpha's Option
The Enforcer's Gamble
The Omega's Prize

◞◟

ABOUT THE AUTHOR

New York Times and *USA Today* bestselling author Vivian Arend loves to share the products of her over-active imagination with her readers. She writes contemporary, western, and light-hearted paranormal romances. The stories are humorous yet emotional, usually with a large cast of family or friends, and a guaranteed happily-ever-after. Vivian lives in British Columbia, Canada, with her husband of many years—her inspiration for every hero and a willing companion for all sorts of adventures.

www.vivianarend.com

www.ingramcontent.com/pod-product-compliance
Lightning Source LLC
Chambersburg PA
CBHW030956210726
48290CB00007B/2328